Measure Twice

J.J. Hensley

To Xia,

Best wishes.

Published by Bad Day Books, an imprint of
Assent Publishing

It's about time somebody gave Hannibal Lecter a run for his money. Lester Mayton, the serial killer who sets new standards of murderous inventiveness in J.J. Hensley's new novel "Measure Twice," is up to the task. Hensley walks a reader right up the edge of unbearable dread, then leavens it with flashes of witty insights into the way local bureaucracies and political infighting can hamper something even as critical as the need to stop a killer before he strikes again.

- Gwen Florio, award-winning author of
Montana and Dakota

J.J. Hensley keeps you turning the pages from the very start. A finely crafted story of redemption, *MEASURE TWICE* will keep your adrenaline pumping.

-Tim Green, bestselling author of *The Forth Perimeter and Exact Revenge*

For Kasia and Cassie

Measure twice, **cut once.**
  -Proverb

THE 12 STEPS TO RECOVERY

Step 1 – We admitted we were powerless over our addiction, that our lives had become unmanageable.

Step 2 – We came to believe that a Power greater than ourselves could restore us to sanity.

Step 3 – We made a decision to turn our will and our lives over to the care of God as we understood Him.

Step 4 – We made a searching and fearless moral inventory of ourselves.

Step 5 – We admited to God, to ourselves, and to another human being the exact nature of our wrongs.

Step 6 – We were entirely ready to have God remove all these defects of character.

Step 7 – We humbly asked Him to remove our shortcomings.

Step 8 – We made a list of all persons we had harmed and became willing to make amends to them all.

Step 9 – We made direct amends to such people wherever possible, except when to do so would injure them or others.

Step 10 – We continued to take personal inventory and when we were wrong promptly admitted it.

Step 11 – We sought through prayer and meditation to improve our conscious contact with God as we understood Him, praying only for knowledge of His will for us and the power to carry that out.

Step 12 – Having had a spiritual awakening as a result of these steps, we tried to carry this message to addicts, and to practice these principles in all our affairs.

PROLOGUE

*H*ell with the lid off. Lester Mayton could not remember who had once described the city that way. He thought it had something to do with the suffocating pollution the populace inhaled in a time when furnaces and factories heated the region's economy, but he was not sure. Whoever had uttered those words would be shocked if he could see the stars draped over the modern skyline tonight. The peaceful buzz reverberating from downtown was in some ways more tranquil than actual silence. It was as if, after decades of relentless forging and hammering, a balance between industry and civility had met right where the rivers converged.

Mayton shifted his weight as the wobbling boat swayed under his feet. He looked toward a towboat that was pushing a barge. Why a boat that pushes something would be called a *tow*boat was a mystery to him. Mayton's eyes narrowed as he tried to focus on the pilot's face that was faintly illuminated by the craft's controls. The pilot glanced in his direction and nodded as the barge moved past the much smaller boat. Mayton waited for the wake of the barge to reach him and absorbed the rocking while watching the skyline rise and fall.

Cindy had loved doing this—sitting out on the river at night and letting the water sway her troubles away. They had both loved this. They had both loved Pittsburgh. They had both loved each other. Now she was gone and this city was to blame. He had tried to stop it. He had done everything in his power, but it was not enough. God often answered prayers, but this city of atheists stopped calling out to the Almighty long ago. The inhabitants had bled faith for decades and the loss had allowed them to drift into a state of numbness in which they did not even realize they were dying. Apathy had taken Cindy away so apathy was the enemy. And the enemy had to be destroyed.

Mayton looked at the gold crucifix in his right hand and then looked into the sky. He had listened to God all of his life. Although he knew he was not perfect, he had never strayed from the path of righteousness. Even when Cindy begged him not to, he donated most of their money to the church. Whenever Cindy started to lose her way, he insisted they spend more time doing volunteer work. When she got sick, he took her to a retreat and pumped her full of the best holistic remedies. She said he was obsessed. Toward the end, she said he was a *God addict*. He knew he was a *believer*. Mayton had tried to be good. Good acts—always. He *had* to do well unto others. But the others did not do well enough in return. Then they took her away from him.

They did not listen to him.

They did not listen to God.

An act of awakening was needed.

As the boat stopped rocking and calmness settled back on the river, Mayton had a brief moment of peace. His eyes moved upward and he took in all that was above him.

They would listen soon. He would make sure of that.

And they would remember.

Remember the atrocities he intended to commit.

But first, he had to break free from his addiction.

— — —

Jackson Channing took a step back from the bathroom mirror and looked at the reflection of his torso. What he saw was a shade of his former self. So many scars. So much damage. When it occurred to him that he had no idea what time it was, he felt depressed. When it occurred to him that he had no idea what day it was, he started to cry. What he did next was predictable. The act had been repeated more times than he could remember. His oily fingerprints were visible all over the clear bottle of whiskey on the nightstand. He added another set as he took a long pull from the container. It did not even burn any more. How could whiskey no longer burn?

The bed creaked as he sat down. When he roughly put the bottle back on the nightstand, everything shook and the framed photo fell over. Picking it up and holding it in his lap, he wondered if she was happier. She had to be; she was not with him. Quickly, he snatched the bottle and took another drink. He had driven her away. He drove everyone away. Dozens of stitches had held his body together, but his sanity had unraveled. It had come undone in that dingy basement. The man who gave him the scars had seen to that. Now all he had left was wreckage.

Channing looked at the clock beside him. It was after ten in the morning. Since he was still on administrative leave from work, he really had nowhere he needed to be. This was going to be his life—purposeless mornings soaked in alcohol.

He started crying again. Then, he took another long pull from the bottle. His supervisors with the Pittsburgh Police Department had told him to take all the time he needed. He needed time all right. He needed time back. He needed Mary back, but that book was closed. One hollow point round in the brain and maybe he could get it all back. Maybe he would get another chance in another life. Perhaps that was the only way.

He opened the drawer of the nightstand and withdrew his pistol. It was loaded. It was always loaded. The GLOCK never failed him. Throughout a ten-year career, probably a hundred thousand rounds had gone through that barrel, obliterating innocent paper targets. Now he would fire one meaningful round. Why not?

Staring at the photo one more time, Channing put the gun in his mouth, closed his eyes, tasted the polymer barrel, felt the front sights scrape against the top of his mouth, and pulled the trigger. The hard click vibrated to the back of his throat. Then…nothing. He opened his eyes. The rear sights were still staring him down. The photo was still in his other hand. He was not breathing, but not because he could not. The only result from his action was the arrival of a cold stillness, nothing but silence surrounding the wreckage. Taking the gun out of his mouth, he looked at it in disbelief. When he pulled back on the slide, a silver round ejected and bounced off his foot. The gun had been loaded. It should have worked. He should be dead. He was not.

Staring at the unspent round which lay by his foot, he felt a glimmer of…of what? Not hope, but something else. A long-forgotten primal instinct for survival? A trace of strength somewhere in his shroud of solitude? Whatever it was, for the moment he was relieved he was not dead. He became conscious of the air filling his lungs, and it did not sadden him. Channing did not think he had the ability to pull the trigger again. The moment was gone. So, if he was not going to end it all this morning, then…what?

The bottle of whiskey and his cell phone sat inches from each other. Channing thought of all of the things he had done. The person he should have been. The person he was not. Then, for the first time in a long time he thought about what he could be. What he still could be. How do you find redemption for your sins? The answer came to him. You don't. You earn it. You have to earn it every day.

With tear-filled eyes he reached toward his nightstand and put the photo of Mary back in its place. Channing was not sure he believed in a higher power. You were born, you lived, and then you died. That was the nature of things. He tried to comprehend what had just happened, and then he reached for the first step toward his salvation. The phone felt small in his hand.

He knew what he had to do now.

He had to earn it.

He needed to wake up.

As soon as the echo of the trigger pull faded away, Channing felt a spark of purpose.

He had to pay attention to the signs. He had to listen to fate.

He would commit acts of redemption that would erase his memories.

But first, he had to break free from his addiction.

STEP 1

**We admitted we were powerless over our addiction, that
our lives had become unmanageable.**

Mayton needed to pull himself together. Mornings were always the worst. His normal routine used to be to head to work and then volunteer at an outreach center, but he would not do either anymore. Cindy's life insurance meant he did not have to have a regular job for quite some time. He would keep up with some other volunteer work on the weekends, only because it fit into his plans.

The one-time Quality Control Manager for a pharmaceutical company knew he was hooked on reciting and living by the words in The Book. To do God's true will he would have to break his habits. Much like Abraham was told to sacrifice his son, Mayton had to sacrifice his faith. The irony was not intended to be understood by a simple mind such as his. Mayton's constant need to give all he had to those around him, and to cherish all life, dominated his existence and now it was time for him to act purely on behalf of his Lord by distancing himself from Him.

One hour of lifting weights and jumping rope was how his days started now. In the beginning, after they took her, he could barely get himself out of bed, much less exercise. The sun coming in his bedroom window only served to illuminate his despair and keep him pinned firmly beneath his blanket. Now, even at forty-five years of age, he could bench press more than most twenty-year-olds. Although he tried to clear his head of prayers, he found himself reciting scripture every time he lifted the weights off his chest. He could stop *doing* good, but he could not yet stop *saying* good. He did not employ creative interpretations of biblical verses to meet his needs. If there was one thing that sickened him to no end, it was the way extremists of the Christian and Muslim faiths would pick and choose specific lines of text, take them out of context, and manipulate the meaning of those words to fit their goals. Muslim terrorists never seemed to mention that Mohammed said, "There is no compulsion in religion," the same way those right-wing militia nuts that claimed to be Christians failed to remember *Matthew 7:1*, "Judge not, that you be not judged."

As hard as he tried not to recite The Book, he was not there yet. If that made him a hypocrite, then so be it. He knew he had been out of control in the past and still could not stop completely. He would have to take baby steps, then he could alter his mind enough to do what had to be done.

Mayton showered, shaved, and made coffee. Sitting at his kitchen table, he combed through the morning paper, finding nothing but bad news. When he finished reading the paper, he was surprised to find the gold crucifix on the table. Picking it up, he stared at it as it twirled from a thin gold chain. He did not remember picking it up from the top of the dresser this morning. He looked at the walls of his kitchen and the hallway that led into the living room. Religious symbolism was everywhere. Wooden and gold crosses hung besides prints of *The Last Supper* and various other works of art. His personal favorite, *The Last Judgment* was situated over the fireplace. Something about that painting always comforted him. The rage displayed on the face of St. Bartholomew while he held a knife in one hand and his own flayed skin in the other was a reminder that wrongs must be revisited and remembered. Victims must be avenged so future generations can sleep soundly. All of the other symbols would have to come down, but not that one. That one could stay.

Mayton put the crucifix down on the table and walked to the closet to get his coat. He walked out the door, got into his car, and started the engine. A minute later, the front door of the house swung open, Mayton rushed to the kitchen, picked up his cross, knelt for a quick prayer, and closed his eyes. When his eyes opened again, he was shocked to see that thirty minutes had passed. A feeling of panic filled his body. There were things he had to prepare before this evening. He could not be late in taking his first step toward redemption. He could not let them hurt someone—again.

– – –

Channing entered the police station and felt entombed by the stares from his colleagues. The second he started walking down the aisle between the desks of his fellow detectives, the shuffling of papers stopped, conversations were left dangling from linguistic cliffs, the room fell silent as a wet blanket of interest suffocated him. Illogically, Channing had a sickening feeling that they could all hear the alcohol being secreted through his pores.

Sergeant Ken Harris's nondescript office was in the back corner of the squad room. The sergeant sounded awkward when Channing called him two hours earlier and told the fifteen-year veteran that he wanted to return to duty. Harris's uncertain tone did not come from any oversensitivity to Channing's plight, but rather from not knowing how to deal with what was sure to be a disruption in the Homicide Squad.

Channing raised his closed fist to the door and watched a tremor reverberate through his bones. He paused and waited for it to pass. He badly needed a drink.

The knock on the door was met with an abrupt, "Come in."

When Channing entered, Harris's shoulders seemed to sag a bit and the mood of the room immediately softened. Harris stood, faced his much taller subordinate, and extended his hand.

"Jackson, it's good to see you."

Channing covertly wiped the sweaty palm of his hand on his pants before reaching out to meet his supervisor's greeting.

Channing opened his mouth to speak, but suddenly worried about his breath and felt the dryness in his throat. In the end, all he could do was nod.

Harris took his seat and gestured toward the empty chair across the desk, but Channing remained standing.

Clearing his throat, Channing tried to imitate the subtle confidence he once had and said, "I'm ready to come back."

"So I gathered from what you said on the phone. Look, nobody would blame you if you took some more time off. Hell, nobody would blame you if you retired on disability and headed off to relax on some beach. You've done your duty. You don't owe anybody anything."

"Except Alex."

Harris fell silent remembering Channing's young and vibrant partner.

Harris dipped his head, stared at a souvenir coffee mug on his desk and said, "Nobody holds you responsible for that. You have to know that."

Channing remained silent and waited for Harris's eyes to once again meet his. He felt his hands begin to shake again and put them in the pockets of his leather jacket. Not knowing how much longer he could keep it together, Channing sped up the conversation.

"I want to be reinstated—today. I want to come back."

"Why don't you give it another couple of weeks?" Harris pleaded. Your desk will still be here."

Now it was Channing's turn to drop his eyes to the desk.

"I *need* to be reinstated. I *have* to come back."

Harris sat quietly for half a minute and finally said, "All right. You work the two-to-ten shift tonight. You'll just be on call until I can reassign some cases to you. Krenshaw is off today, but you'll partner up with him starting tomorrow."

"No partner," blurted Channing way too quickly.

"It doesn't work that way and you know it," Harris replied.

"I need to work alone for a while. Besides, I'm sure Krenshaw would rather work with somebody else."

Harris's face hardened a bit. "This isn't a negotiation. You go solo tonight, but tomorrow you and Krenshaw pair up. If I put you out there on your own, the brass will eat me alive if—"

"If I fuck up," Channing interrupted.

Harris did not respond.

Channing felt beads of sweat start to form on his

forehead, and his hands seemed to be independent of the rest of his nervous system. This office had never seemed small to him before, but now it was oppressive. His lungs needed more air. He had to get out of the room.

"I'll be back this afternoon," Channing said, then hesitantly added, "And I'll need a new GLOCK issued to me. I need to get mine checked out by the armorer. I think something is wrong with it."

"No problem," replied the sergeant with a trace of apprehension. "I'll call down to property and you can pick it up before your shift."

Channing opened the door and began walking out. He paused, then without looking back, said, "Thanks, Ken. I mean it." Then he left and closed the door behind him.

This time the gauntlet of detectives was ready for him. Several of them approached him and mumbled greetings. Some slurred out condolences. Whether the condolences were because of him losing his partner, his wife, or due to his ordeal, he did not know. Channing shook several hands, each dryer than his, then quickly proceeded toward the nearest restroom.

After flinging a stall door open and then slamming it closed, Channing frantically reached inside his jacket and pulled out a silver flask. The vodka was not exactly odorless, as people tended to say, but it would have to do. He poured half the flask down his throat and waited for the shaking to subside. Four minutes later, he exited the stall, walked to the sink, and threw cold water into his bloodshot eyes. Looking up from the porcelain, he once again gazed into the eyes of a man he no longer knew. What had happened to him? How had it gone this far? If he did not learn to control this thing, he was going to make a mistake, and someone would get hurt—again.

— — —

Nicholas Culligan was never late. Not for a meeting, not for a dentist appointment, not for the thorny semi-annual dinners he had with his son. More importantly, in the four years since being elected as the City Council representative for District One, he had never been late for or missed a single council-related function. He turned the corners of the underground parking lot a little too fast and squealed his Lexus into his reserved parking space.

After learning the ropes during his first year in public office, he became chairman of the council's least desirable committee. The Committee for Performance and Asset Management handled the city's contracts, purchases, fleet management, facilities decisions, and information systems. The committee's realm was a bureaucratic wilderness teeming with opportunities for someone to be implicated for bribery, kickbacks, cronyism, and incompetence.

When, at fifty-six years of age, Culligan had decided to run for city council, it was partly out of boredom, but mostly out of necessity. The previous year, he had retired from a local brokerage firm with a healthy portfolio. Several promising investment opportunities were laid out in front of him to help him coast into the golden years. He would simply roam the fairways of the area's golf courses in the summer, head down to Hilton Head in the winter, and enjoy a well-earned respite from the hustle and bustle of the financial world. His ace in the hole was the massive amount of stock he owned in a Detroit-based company called Cityflash, which specialized in urban revitalization projects. Culligan got in on the ground floor of the investment after receiving an inside tip that the company had signed a deal with the city of Detroit. The privileged information came from a cousin who happened to work in the Detroit Mayor's Office. Of course, Culligan knew acting on the information was tantamount to insider trading, but he viewed the financial world as one huge gray area full of mercenaries—and no white knights.

When Cityflash expanded, Culligan's large investment expanded with it. When the company subsequently signed contracts with other dilapidated cities such as Toledo, Youngstown, and Cleveland, he made millions. With no Internet bubble to burst, the investment was the closest thing to a sure bet. Culligan went all-in.

Then the mayor of Detroit was indicted. Leaders in the other cities met similar fates. Charges were filed that contained ugly words like *collusion* and *conspiracy*. The revitalization company that was the darling of the rust belt corroded into scrap metal within a week. The company's CEO was one of dozens of company employees crucified in the media and displayed as examples of corporate greed and corruption. Everything fell apart. Culligan did not go bankrupt by any means, but his dreams of an easy retirement were gone. He tried to get his old job back, but there were whispers that his rise and fall were tied to Cityflash. With nothing left but a shady background and some influential friends whom he had met through the firm, there was only one place for him to turn—politics. His current committee was the perfect way for him to make up his losses and ride off into a sunset much warmer than the current one he was experiencing this Pennsylvania winter. He was almost there. Just one or two more deals and he would be comfortable again.

Culligan grumbled to himself as he got out of the Lexus. He had five minutes to get to the council chambers. He was never late. Opening the rear driver's side door, Culligan reached for the briefcase he knew was there but could not see in the poorly lit garage. Finding the handle, he swiftly yanked the briefcase out of the seat, slammed the door, turned to his right, and heard the thud. He heard the sound before his eyes registered the figure that suddenly appeared right beside him. Culligan was confused. The man was not touching him, but seemed to be holding him up. The councilman tried to cry out, but no sound came. He felt his legs give way, but he did not fall. The figure gently turned him so his back was against the Lexus, and now Culligan could see eyes. The man leaned in close, whispered two barely-perceivable words, and raised his right hand. The assailant waved a weapon in front of Culligan's eyes in a near-hypnotic manner, watched the public official's eyes widen, and then used the weapon as God had intended.

– – –

Seven hours. Channing had made it seven hours. When he arrived to work at two o'clock, the squad room was buzzing with activity. Some of the detectives who had not seen him earlier welcomed him back. A few who did not know how to react simply gave him a nod from across the room. Some, he suspected, were dodging him altogether either out of an avoidance of the incommodious or worse.

While he sat at his desk, Channing tried to catch up on every interdepartmental memo and notification he could. He checked on his old cases to see if they had been handled. Most had, or were simply filed away as unsolved. Only twice did he have to disappear to the restroom and take a drink to keep the shaking away. He had been issued a new weapon and fresh supply of ammunition when he arrived, but he shuttered to think what would happen if he had to fire it with a trembling hand.

At nine o'clock, his desk phone rang. Someone had changed his ringtone. There must have been some intern using the desk in his absence. That would explain the doodling on his desk calendar that was now several months out of date. Channing picked up the phone, listened, and immediately wished he had picked up the bottle that morning rather than his cell phone. He was going to have to go out on a call.

"Don't you recognize him?" said the officer at the scene.

Channing did not respond.

"It's Nick Culligan…as in Councilman Culligan!"

Channing just kept looking at the officer.

"Jackson, are you following me? It's a city councilman. Right there!"

The use of his first name caused Channing to focus on the woman in the uniform. *My God*, he thought. *What's wrong with me?* Her name was Linda Aluseo. He had gone through the academy with her. They were friends once. He and Mary had even gone to a Pirates game with her and her husband. He did not even recognize her. *Focus.*

Taking a breath, Channing asked, "Who found him?"

He immediately felt stupid for asking the question. A better question would have been: *Who **didn't** find him?*

"A guy walking his dog across the Warhol Bridge was the first to call it in. Then it was a free-for-all. We got initial statements from him and a few others that stayed around to gawk. We've got them all down by the museum if you want to talk to them, but all their statements are the same. None of them said they had actually seen how he got there."

Channing looked down beneath his feet. Then, out of the corner of his eye he saw bright lights illuminating the night. The reporters were setting up. There was no way he could handle this. Not the press. No way. He looked back down and remained very silent. He suddenly felt a bit of relief when he realized he had a valid question to ask Aluseo.

"How did you ID him? You can't really see his face from here."

Aluseo pointed down and said, "I didn't. River Rescue did. They used their spotlight and binoculars and recognized him."

Channing looked at her skeptically.

"What can I say?" She shrugged. "They have really good lights."

Shaking his head, Channing replied, "That's not what I was thinking. I'm wondering who in the world knows the faces of the city council."

"Are you kidding me?" Aluseo asked with a slight grin. "Jesus, Jackson, don't you read the papers?"

She immediately fell silent as she caught her mistake.

"I'm sorry, Jackson. I guess you've avoided the news for a while, haven't you?"

Channing did not speak. He felt his hands start to shake and slid them into his pockets.

"Look, I'm not trying to be insensitive. I should have started off by asking how you are doing, telling you how sorry I am about Alex. But knowing how you are, I just figured you'd rather skip all that and get back to work."

A boat motor started up in the distance. More camera

lights appeared to Channing's right and left. More flashing red and blue lights approached from all sides. The rotors of a helicopter thumped above. *Too much. Way too much.* It had to be thirty-five degrees and windy, but he was sweating. He could feel the flask pressing on his heart. He noticed a throbbing sensation through the crisscrossing scar tissue on his chest and back. The scars felt like a web of downed power lines beginning to burn through his skin.

"You're right. I just want to work. And no, I haven't read the papers in a while."

Aluseo adjusted her hat and pushed some black strands of hair underneath it.

After blowing on her cold hands, she said, "Well, Culligan was fighting off some accusations of taking kickbacks from a construction contractor. Some disgruntled employee from the company swore on a stack of bibles that Culligan was dirty and in bed with the company's president. It was in the papers for a couple of weeks and then…poof. I never saw anything more about it. I think I heard that the accuser changed his story, but don't quote me on that."

Channing looked down again. His cell phone started ringing. He knew who it was—Harris. His sergeant probably heard that there was a call-out and that a councilman was involved. Channing catching the case could be a nightmare for everyone involved. Channing pulled the phone out of his pocket. Aluseo, probably sensing Channing's tension, walked away.

"Channing."

"It's Harris. I heard you got a call-out. Whacha got?"

"I haven't confirmed it, but I'm told the vic is Councilman Culligan."

The Sergeant was quiet.

After a few seconds, Channing looked at the phone to see if the call was still active and then said, "Sarge, you there?"

"Did you say the victim is a councilman?"

"Yeah. Guy named Culligan. But like I said, it's not confirmed."

Harris let another long pause hang in the air. This time Channing waited.

Finally, Harris came back with, "Anyone in custody?"

"No—witnesses didn't actually see it happen. They just spotted the body."

"Any chance it was natural causes? A heart attack, stroke, or something like that?"

Channing wished he could say yes. He took the phone away from his face and shivered from the cold wind and the withdraw symptoms. He wished this would all go away. It didn't matter. Harris would reassign the case tomorrow anyway. There was no way he would let Channing touch this one.

Taking in the scene, Channing slowly panned around trying to process the surreal. To his left was a collection of news vans parked next to the baseball stadium. Stretching across in front of him was the Warhol Bridge, full of onlookers who would never stand out on a bridge on a wintry night under any other circumstances. To his right was the downtown skyline. The red and blue lights of emergency vehicles were reflecting off the buildings to create a bizarre Christmassy effect. Above him were media helicopters with their night-cutting spotlights, circling like vultures. And a soulless distance below him was the frigid Allegheny River. The only things between his feet and the near frozen waters were a three-inch-thick metal grate sidewalk, a long rope, and the blood-covered body that dangled from the end of it. The thick rope was attached somewhere below the Clemente Bridge. Standing directly over the point where the rope attached to the bridge, Channing fought back his nausea, tried to steady his hand that held the cell phone, and raised the phone back to his cold, sweat-covered face.

"No. I don't think it's from natural causes."

STEP 2

We came to believe that a Power greater than ourselves could restore us to sanity.

The morning after he delivered justice to Culligan, Mayton woke early and performed his one-hour exercise routine. It was not until after he cleaned up and was drinking coffee at his kitchen table that he realized he had not prayed yet. He had not even recited biblical passages during his workout. Progress.

Mayton thought about the previous night's events. He was certain he had done everything right. When he returned home, he removed and burned all the clothes he was wearing. He stood naked and shivering in his backyard until every last article of clothing turned to ash. He then walked into the outdoor shower he had rigged and scrubbed himself until his skin was bright pink. He did not have any hot water for that shower, but he endured the chill for nearly ten minutes. He did not retain any of his instruments, as they were easy enough to come by. They were somewhere in the bottom of the Allegheny, but far from where he left Culligan hanging.

The only loose end was his old van. He cleaned it as well as he could to eliminate any evidence from Culligan's body, but keeping it was still a risk. The white 1990 Ford Econoline was the only vehicle he owned. He had picked the wreck up at a church auction and fixed it up enough for it to run and pass a state inspection. Mayton refused to spend money on frivolities such as fancy cars. The van was good enough to get him to work and to help deliver food to the sick, so it was good enough.

Now, Mayton wished he owned another car. Cindy had a car as well because of her job, but Cindy's used Honda was a reminder that he did not want to have around. He could not stand the sight of that car and, as soon as she passed, he donated the car to charity. It was a reminder of how he failed her. He would have preferred her to stay at home and raise their children, but children were not in God's plan for the Mayton family. So, Cindy wanted—no, demanded—a career. After enduring several arguments, Lester finally agreed that Cindy would work and she would have her own car. He would have preferred that they carpool, but Cindy worked on the other side of town and argued that wasting money on gas to sit in cross-town traffic in both directions was not logical. When Cindy said they could give that money to the church, Lester became angry, realizing that she was playing on his altruism in order to manipulate him.

Regardless, Cindy took a job in a building near the North Shore. Lester was also hesitant to allow her to work for a government entity, but when his wife told him that she would be working for the Housing Authority to help the needy find homes, he once again relented. She was the most stubborn woman he had ever met, but he loved her dearly.

He had pushed her away by trying to control her. He knew

that now. His constant praying, insistence on giving everything away, and what she called his archaic beliefs drove her to take a job far from his office. The power he felt through prayer and the church dominated his very being. He tried to explain that to her, but all she would say was that she felt power through loving him. Now he understood. There actually were other ways to feel powerful. The previous night in that parking garage, Mayton finally felt it. It shot through him unlike any biblical passage or religious ceremony ever had. When he looked into Culligan's eyes and delivered the overdue retribution, Mayton felt the greatest power of all right in his hands: the power of granting life or dealing death. Things were starting to become clearer.

– – –

Channing did not leave the bridge until early the following morning after the body was discovered. It was only by slipping into his car for a minute on the pretense of having some privacy for a phone call, that he was able to down the rest of the contents of his flask and get a handle on his physiology. The sun had been up for a while when Channing finally finished briefing all the supervisors who rushed to the scene so they could feel important. By the time he returned home, dizziness and the feeling of hopelessness a man typically feels where every single person in the world but him is competent, supplemented his shaking.

Exhausted, walking through his bedroom, Channing stripped off his clothes and headed to the shower. Minutes later, while sitting in the tub and letting the steaming hot water rain on him from above, he started to think about the murder. *Who does something like that? Dangling a body from a bridge in the middle of a city? That's someone making a statement.* Channing had still been at the scene when the fire department arrived and used some sort of device with hooks and pulleys to bring the body up. Each painful process lasted too long. A couple of times when they were bringing the body up to the bridge, the corpse banged loudly off the steel girders that supported the sidewalk, causing more than a few first responders to cringe.

Once the body was on the bridge, it only took a minute for some of the more-knowledgeable city employees to confirm the body was that of Culligan. Channing had noted that the body hadn't been suspended by rope around the neck, but rather by a loop of rope that was tied around the torso. This was a good thing—if Culligan had been thrown off the bridge with a noose around his neck, his head would have probably popped off due, in large part, to the giant gash across his throat. Blood ran completely down the front of Culligan's suit jacket and dress shirt. Another item that drew Channing's attention was a concentration of blood in two areas on Culligan's chest. There appeared to be two large holes in the councilman's chest, each of them just above his nipples.

Channing reached up and adjusted the water temperature higher. *Did someone shoot the guy, slash his throat, and then throw him off a bridge?* There was a lot of blood from the throat gash, indicating Culligan was alive when the cut was made. *So, someone cut his throat, then shot him, and then threw him off a bridge? That was not just someone making a statement; that was wrath.* He had to stop thinking about it. He was not ready to deal with a major case. This was not his problem. He would turn over the case notes to Harris and let him assign one of the other detectives. Hell, it was probably already reassigned and his day-shift colleagues were out there starting from scratch because they would not trust Channing's notes anyway. He needed a drink.

Toweling off, Channing walked back into his bedroom and thought about the rope. The first witnesses called 9-1-1 at 9:03 p.m. That was still a fairly busy time in the downtown area, even on a cold weekday night. *How did someone put a body on a rope tied to a support beam under the bridge, toss it off the bridge, and get away without being noticed? And where was Culligan killed? There were only a few smears of blood on the railing of the walkway. He had to have been killed somewhere else.* Laying back on the bed, Channing thought about having to walk into that squad room in a few hours and having pity-filled eyes watch him enter Harris's office to hand over the notes on a case that was currently out of his league. He needed a drink.

When he was leaving the scene, the day-shift detectives were heading over to the City Council Chambers to see if Culligan had reported to work yesterday. *Did he have a council meeting that evening? Did he drive? Where was his car? If he was, in fact, dirty, how many enemies did this guy have?* Channing closed his eyes and lined up the questions in his mind, and drifted off to sleep. Things were starting to become clearer.

He forgot that he needed a drink.

– – –

Channing could see a silhouette pacing through the frosted glass of Harris's closed door. Occasionally, the muffled sound of raised voices rose above the squad room's white noise of ringing, clicking, and conversing. Channing sat at his desk staring at the door with his notebook in his hands, eager to rid himself of the previous night's ugliness. He had fallen asleep submerged in questions, but woke up to the usual unbearable thirst. Three vodkas later, he was able to right himself enough to make it to the station.

Channing slowly dragged his thumb down the metal spirals of his notebook and listened to the calming sound it made change ever so slightly from the top spirals to the bottom ones. He mindlessly repeated the action a few more times, letting each spiral have its own moment. Suddenly, the image of a naked spine full of bloody vertebrae flashed before him. The image turned his stomach. He dropped the notebook on the desk, quickly rose, and rushed to the restroom.

After vomiting the contents of his stomach, Channing refilled it with a few swigs of Smirnoff and popped a breath mint in his mouth. By the time he returned to the squad room, Harris's door was open and the sergeant was scanning the room. Upon spotting Channing, he made a beckoning motion and turned away. Channing walked to his desk, picked up his notebook, and headed over to his supervisor's office.

Harris was not alone. Sitting in a chair opposite a large faux-oak desk was one of the squad's three female detectives, Tina Lambert. She stared at the souvenir coffee mug sitting on Harris's desk and did not look up to meet Channing's eyes when he walked into the room. From his angle, Channing could see a stern expression on her face and a clinched jaw. He assumed she was the owner of the pacing silhouette he viewed earlier. Harris greeted Channing and gestured toward an empty chair next to Lambert.

Harris spoke first.

"Well, I'll get right to the point. It's been decided that Tina will take the lead on the Culligan case."

Channing nodded and waited for more.

"I've explained to her that the only reason you aren't the lead on this one is because you've been out so long. Otherwise—"

"No problem. I understand," Channing interrupted while lifting his notebook and attempting to hand it to Lambert.

"You can hold on to that," Harris said in a tone tinged with reservation. "You're working with her on the case."

Channing slowly lowered the notebook back into his lap and looked at Harris who was now expressionless.

"You can't be serious."

The sergeant, who always reduced everything to the bare facts when he felt stress, kept his voice even.

"I am. Lambert will be the lead, you'll back her up, and Terio and Belton will assist as needed."

"Ken, I…like you said, I just came back."

"That's the way it is. You've cleared dozens of homicides. This one isn't any different."

"The hell it isn't!" Channing was surprised to hear his own raised voice and immediately lowered his volume. He glanced at Lambert who was still scrutinizing the coffee mug, and then returned his gaze to his supervisor. "Can we speak alone for a minute?"

That caught Lambert's attention and she impatiently broke in, "Yeah, why don't you two talk and I'll get to work." She stood up, obviously not wanting to be there in the first place.

Harris started to say something to her and then his eyes gave permission for her to leave. When the door closed behind Lambert, Harris leaned back in his chair and seemed to relax a little.

"It's not my call, Jackson. You're on this thing. No choice."

"Why? Anybody could work with Lambert. You wanted to pair me up with Krenshaw. Let me go work with him and pair Lambert up with someone else."

"I'm telling you, it's not my call. In fact, the original plan was that you would be the lead detective on the case. I suggested Terio get it instead. In the end it was decided that Lambert would lead, but you would have to be involved."

"Jesus, Ken. I'm in no shape for this. And Lambert's got what…a year in the squad? Why the fu—"

Then it came to him.

"Because of the press? Are you kidding me? Tell me it's not because of the press, Ken. Tell me I'm wrong."

Now Harris was staring at the coffee mug. Channing had a fleeting thought that with the attention it was getting, the thing must have been the most interesting freaking drinking device since the Holy Grail.

Harris looked back at Channing and sighed. "You're still big news. The press saw you at the scene. If the department doesn't put its hero cop on the case, there will be too many questions."

Hero cop. Channing's right hand trembled a bit.

"You know that's bullshit."

"Don't say any more." Harris held a hand up, afraid of what the detective would say next. "Those were the chief's words, not mine." Then the supervisor looked at his subordinate awkwardly. "I'm not saying you aren't a hero. I'm…I'm just saying that the press labeled you that way, so in the eyes of the brass, you are. Nobody has the right to judge you for whatever happened in that house. If I would have been in your shoes…well, who knows?"

"And Lambert?"

Harris shrugged.

Channing looked at the ceiling and answered his own question.

"Who better to pair with the fucking *hero cop* then a young, ambitious, African-American, female detective who was a track and field star at Duquesne?"

The sergeant started to speak and then stopped. He took in a deep breath and simply uttered, "Like I said. Not my call. And Tina's a good detective. You know that. She's just a little more focused on career advancement than I'd like."

Channing stood. Now it was his turn to pace the small room.

"This isn't a career maker! It's a career killer! Did you tell her that? Best-case...and I mean *best*-case scenario, we catch whoever killed Culligan. When it goes to trial, everything Culligan did to wrong this guy is going to come out. Then everything Culligan ever did to *anyone* is going to come out. Culligan will be demonized and the police will be viewed as the defenders of a corrupt politician. If the suspect has money, then the trial could last years. It's a train wreck waiting to happen."

"What are you talking about? Why are you assuming Culligan was deliberately targeted because of something he did to someone? And stop pacing around, you're making me dizzy!"

Channing kept walking.

"Come on. The guy was killed with two shots to the chest, had his throat cut, then he was strung up on the Clemente Bridge and displayed for the entire city to see. This wasn't some robbery gone bad. This was premeditated, calculated, and purposeful. This is vengeance personified. Add in a dash of politics, a few lawyers, and this is a powder keg sitting next to the devil's fireplace."

Harris gave a half-grin.

"That's why Tina will need your help. You see things that a lot of people can't see, and don't *want* to see."

Channing sat down again, put his elbows on his knees, and looked at the floor. Several solemn seconds passed before Harris spoke again.

"You're right about one thing and you're wrong about two. You're right that Lambert's not ready for this."

Not wanting to ask the obvious, Channing raised his head enough to make eye contact with his sergeant.

"But I think you're wrong about you not being ready."

Channing dropped his head again. Was his hand trembling?

"And you're wrong about Culligan being shot."

Now, every part of Channing's body was still.

— — —

"Good afternoon, Lester."

Mayton put on his best smile as he walked through the gate.

"How are you doing, Rick?"

The eighty-year-old man was holding the reins of a brown horse and leading it to a stable.

"Oh, just feelin' the cold a bit, but I'm doin' just fine."

Mayton exchanged smiles and short pleasantries with a few other people as he made his way down the dirt road. The scent of burning wood filled the air and resurrected a childhood memory. His father spent hours splitting wood. The man's hands—and his personality—were strong and calloused. He could take on any task for hours on end and never once complain.

Five hours without prayer. Five hours. The drive there was the toughest. In the van, there was not much else to do than think and pray. He avoided the religious programs on the radio and found some classic rock station. When a song came on that invited the listener to smoke a joint and get undressed, Mayton instinctually reached for the button that would change the station, but stopped himself. He forced himself to listen to the music until the end of the song and then shut the radio off. For the remainder of the trip, rather than fill his mind with prayer, he worked through the steps he would need to take to continue with his mission.

His hands stung from the wind. It was a short walk from the van to his workplace. The area had hardly seen any snow this winter, but the bitter air sweeping down the rivers made every journey outside an uncomfortable experience. Once inside the cabin, he raced over and got a fire going. He warmed his hands and looked around the quiet space. He doubted he would have any visitors today. Just as well. He was always able to achieve a great deal of focus when left alone.

The cabin—if that was the right word for it—did not belong to him, but it may as well have. In this place, Mayton let his mind roam free while forcing his hands to perform their solemn duty. Everything was as it had been when he worked in quality control. Mayton thought about the similarities to his old job. *Every movement had to be precise. Every moment was calculated. Little was wasted and nothing was lost.* He remembered the strategy he had so often preached to others. *With the analysis of any process, a predictable failure rate can be ascertained. By eliminating variability in the process, defects are eliminated and a successful outcome becomes likely.* How many times had he followed Culligan into that parking garage in past months? Four? Five? He had planned every detail. A rare grin crossed Mayton's lips. *It's Six-Sigma in the deadliest sense,* he thought.

His hands still hovered over the fire. He made fists, then stretched out his fingers. *So much power to create,* he thought. *So much power to destroy.* He knew he would do both simultaneously, but it had to be done correctly. The process would be adhered to and he must do his best to keep his emotions in check. He flexed his fingers and let the heat loosen his stiff knuckles. The crackling of wood filled his ears. There was something special about sitting in front of a fire. It, too, could create or destroy.

STEP 3

We made a decision to turn our will and our lives over to the care of God *as we understood Him.*

Tina Lambert was sitting at her desk when Channing emerged from the office. Not knowing what to say, he started to walk to his own desk, then realized he had no reason to go there. Sizing up the situation, he decided to address things head-on. That was how he was before his extended absence; maybe he could be that way again. She raised her eyes when he reached her desk.

"Good talk?" she asked in a tone somewhere between sarcasm and resentment.

"Not particularly."

The senior detective shifted his weight from one leg to the other.

"Well, where do you want to start?"

The way she asked that question left no doubt about it. There was some real resentment present. Channing could not blame her. If he were in her place, he certainly would not want to work with him. He was tainted and no matter how many times people tried to hang the *hero* label on him, most of the department knew the truth, even if they did not want to admit it.

With a senior detective looking over her shoulder, Lambert was also sure to feel as if she was being micromanaged. Channing was certain Lambert was sensing a power struggle on the horizon. Having navigated many territorial battles before, Channing felt he knew how to get past most of these. *The funny thing is*, he thought, *I do not even want to win the battle*. Hell…he did not even want any of the territory. He just had to accept the assignment because his two options were to work, or to…to what?

"Look, you heard Harris. You're in charge. I've been out of things a while, so I'm just following your lead."

"Uh huh," Lambert replied while scribbling some notes, indicating she was completely unconvinced.

"After I left the scene, I went home and crashed for a few hours, so I'm not really up to speed. Do you think we could go over my notes and you could fill me in on any new information?"

The wiry woman shuffled some papers on her desk and sighed.

"Sure. Why not? Let's go into the conference room."

On the way to the conference room, Channing poured himself a cup of coffee from a pot sitting in the corner of the squad room. The first sip he took made his stomach do a somersault and, by the time they reached the conference room door, he had deposited his Styrofoam cup in the trash can. For the life of him, he could not figure out why police station coffee always tasted like stale battery acid. The burnt taste stuck with him as he and Lambert took seats at a large rectangular table.

Lambert had barely moved her chair toward the table when she started speaking. Once again, she seemed to avoid looking at her new partner.

"I got the summary you left with the day-shift guys, so I'm not sure what else you want to cover from your notes."

"I guess I probably know a lot less than you do at this point."

Now she looked at him, and it was not a pleasant look.

"Don't patronize me, okay?"

"Excuse me?"

"Don't fucking patronize me. Just tell me what you want to know."

Channing swallowed hard and was the first to break eye contact. He stammered a bit and then struggled to organize his thoughts. My God, how things had changed. A few months ago, if anyone, especially a junior detective, had talked to him that way, he would have eaten them alive. Not long ago, he was considered by some to be a bit cocky. A certain level of arrogance was required in order to do the job well. In a profession where unconcealed egotism was everywhere, Channing had a reputation for being extremely confident, but not to the point of recklessness.

Not everybody liked him. He was not that type of guy. But everyone respected him. His degree in psychology from Wake Forest and his hobby of running marathons gave many of his old-school, beer-guzzling colleagues pause, but he usually softened them up with a quiet competence and good sense of humor. He had stepped on a few toes over the years, but up until the previous May, nobody had questioned his work performance or his judgment. Then he let his partner and best friend, Alex Belmont, go into that house. Then he killed Alex.

"I suppose you want to know where Culligan was killed." Lambert was still looking at him, but some of the fire was out of her eyes. In fact, there was an appearance of concerned perplexity on her face. How long had he been silent? Seconds? Minutes?

"Yeah. That would be…yeah."

The woman leaned back in her chair and maintained a business-like demeanor, but it was obvious she was no longer on the attack. She seemed to be puzzled by Channing's lack of a defense. She had poked the bear and the bear retreated. That was not what she expected.

Lambert took a deep breath and sized up the man across from her. Maybe she was not being completely fair to him. From what she knew of Jackson Channing, he was a good guy who did not shy away from tough assignments. She had to consider that her abrasiveness was unwarranted, but she had learned to be watchful. She had come too far in her life to let her ambitions get derailed by yet another white man in the department who had no idea what it was like to have to break through multiple glass ceilings. However, she had to admit, this guy had a sense of sincerity about him that most men in the department lacked.

With some amount of hesitation, she said, "The lower level of a parking garage on Forbes. He had a space there for when he was visiting the Council Chambers."

"So he was working yesterday."

"Yeah. The council was scheduled to have a session and a vote at four o'clock. It looks like Culligan parked his car and got ambushed. The day-shift guys found blood everywhere next to, and on, his car. It was pretty messy."

"Witnesses?"

"None. And no cameras on that level, but there are

cameras recording vehicles going in and out of the garage. The disc is back at my desk. I was going to go over it tonight."

Channing nodded. He was freezing. A minute earlier he was fine. *Great*, he thought. *Sweating outside and freezing inside.* The burnt taste from the coffee got stronger.

"Do you mind if I watch it with you?" he asked.

With a shrug, Lambert mumbled, "Suit yourself."

"Did anyone report Culligan missing? His wife?"

"He didn't have any close family. Divorced. Lived alone. His ex-wife and adult son were notified. Neither of them had talked to Culligan in weeks. Terio went out there. He said they didn't seem too torn up when they got the news. Councilman Hatton called Chief Blakely this morning. He said all the council members were surprised when Culligan didn't show up. Apparently, the guy had a thing about punctuality. He was OCD about it or something. None of them called the police, but Hatton said that he did try to call Culligan's cell phone. The forensics guys found a cell on Culligan when they processed the body. There were three missed calls from Hatton."

Now, Channing felt hot again. A few more minutes and he would have to escape to the bathroom and dig out his flask to steady himself.

"Before I left the bridge this morning, I asked the zone sergeant to have his guys comb the area for surveillance and traffic cameras on the surrounding buildings. Did they have any luck?"

"No traffic cam on the bridge, but the stadium had cameras on the north end of the bridge and there is a camera on the south end, keeping an eye on a rental car place. It captures part of Sixth Street leading up to the south end of the bridge. I have all of those recordings at my desk, too."

Channing perked up a bit.

"That's great! We can compare the footage from the parking garage and the two cameras around the bridge and see if the same car shows up in both of them."

Lambert took a pen, scribbled something in her notepad, and then said, "Did the sarge tell you about the holes?"

"Yes. I assumed they were gunshots, but he said they were puncture wounds."

Clicking the pen in her left hand, she simply responded with another, "Uh huh."

"Any idea when the medical examiner will have more information for us?"

She was partially absent now. After a beat, she responded with, "Na. Probably tomorrow."

Channing watched as Lambert clicked her pen three more times and kept her gaze on her notepad. *What was she thinking?*

He moved on to his next question.

"Forensics?"

"Probably a preliminary report tomorrow. High-profile. They'll put a rush on it, but the lab work and final analysis will take some time."

The young detective gave three more clicks and finally put the notepad down. Whatever was on her mind seemed to have resolved itself for the time being.

Looking at Channing, Lambert refocused on the task at hand.

"The man was a politician. I'm sure he pissed some people off, right? I figure we should talk to the other council members, find out who he screwed over, and see if he received any threats. The department doesn't have a record of any, but maybe the council didn't call them in."

"So, you don't think this was random? Maybe a robbery gone bad?" Channing asked.

Anger appeared in the younger detective's eyes again. Maybe she had misread this guy and he *was* just like the others.

"Are you kidding me? Is that supposed to be funny?"

Channing shook his head, confused. Was he that out of touch when it came to dealing with other people? He did not seem to be able to get a read on this woman. She had only been with the squad for a few months before Channing went on leave. He did not have much of a chance to get to know her, so maybe she was always this bipolar.

"No. I'm not kidding. And I'm not being funny. I really want your opinion."

"A fucking City Councilman gets his lungs punctured, his throat gashed open, and then suspended from a bridge in the middle of downtown for God and everyone to see, and you're asking me if it's random?"

For the first time that day, Channing smiled. Maybe being partnered with this woman would be a good thing. He would just have to keep trying to find their common ground and have a little faith.

— — —

Tedla Abdella did not deserve this. He had overcome too much, come too far, to have this be his closing chapter. When people referred to him, they used terms like "The American Dream" and talked about the "land of opportunity". No, he did not deserve this.

At the age of eight, he and his family escaped the war-torn country of Eritrea. By the age of eleven, he had learned

English. By sixteen, he was at the top of his class. By eighteen, he received an academic scholarship to Carnegie Mellon University. Upon graduating with two degrees from Carnegie Mellon's School of Engineering and Public Policy, he was primed to hook up with one of the big computer companies in Silicon Valley. When the Internet bubble burst, he got into land development. When the housing bubble burst, he looked for a more stable profession.

In the eleven years he served as the Executive Director for the Pittsburgh Housing Authority, he accomplished a great deal. The city was a model of revitalization and renovation. The city's low-income housing was not going to be mistaken for affluent subdivisions, but they were not the dangerous slums that existed at the beginning of his tenure. Having risen out of poverty, he enjoyed helping those who wished to do the same. He knew his heart was in the right place. Even if he had to bend a few rules or cut a few questionable deals, it was all for the greater good. The new Housing Authority office building near the North Shore was just one example of how far the agency had come.

A subdued tapping brought him back to the present. Not a tapping, but the sound of drops of liquid striking unsympathetic cement, their rhythm reminiscent of a lethargic metronome keeping the beat of an unnamed, doleful song.

Blood from his fingertips dripped down to the floor. He was not sure where he was, but he knew he was in trouble. He assumed someone would find his car on the gravel road near his secluded North Hills home. His wife would call the police when he did not show up by...when? Seven? Eight? What time was it now? Was it even the same day?

Abdella had been slightly surprised to see the old white

van with the hood up blocking the narrow road near his home. There were only a few homes off that road and he knew all of the residents and their cars. Knowing nobody in that section of the North Hills would be caught dead driving a heap like that, he assumed that one of his neighbors must have hired a contractor of some sort. He envied whatever neighbor was able to get a contractor out this way on a Saturday evening. From the looks of things, the van had broken down and the driver was not able to pull off to the side. No big deal. Abdella, on his way back from his usual Saturday massage, would help the smiling man who stood next to the vehicle push it off to the side.

When Abdella had positioned himself behind the van in order to push, he called up to the contractor who had gotten in behind the wheel and told him to release the break. When the man did not answer, Abdella peeked around the driver's side of the van and yelled again. He had expected to see the contractor's face in the side view mirror, but all he saw was the headrest of the driver's seat. Abdella yelled again, confused. The man did not appear to be in the van anymore. The head of the Housing Authority started to take a step forward in the direction of the driver's door, but a small voice in his head told him to stop. He felt a twinge of panic and a quick burst of adrenaline; maybe it was the remnants of some overly developed sense of survival he still carried with him from the homeland. His feet hurt. It was an unusual thing he remembered from his childhood. His feet always hurt when his guard suddenly went up.

Abdella slowly stepped backwards, retreating to the back corner of the van. He kept his eyes forward, hoping that the driver would reappear in the mirror. When Abdella's retreat took him past the rear taillight of the van, he tensed up and saw a flurry of motion to his right. That was the last thing he remembered prior to waking up in this room.

Whatever the man had hit him in the head with was heavy and effective. Now, tied to this old wooden chair by what seemed like entire spools of fishing line cutting into his wrists and ankles, he again wondered what he had done to deserve this.

The man from the road did not look menacing. Abdella knew what evil looked like. Even though he was young at the time, he remembered seeing the faces of evil. They bore bloodshot eyes filled with rage and carried rusty machetes. Yes, he knew what evil looked like. This man did not have the look. In fact, at the time, the man had looked…serene. He looked…dead calm. Coming to this realization, the prisoner felt something hard form in the pit of his stomach. He suddenly felt very sick. This was not evil that Abdella had seen before, but it was, in fact, a deliberate evil. The man who had posed as a contractor was standing at a workbench with his back to Abdella. *And was he…was he whistling?* Abdella thought he recognized the tune. Something with a title like *That Old Time Religion.* The clinking of metal parts echoed in what could have been a basement. *Wait*, Abdella thought. It *was* a basement. He knew this place.

The man, still whistling, turned toward Abdella. Only the lower part of the stranger's torso was visible. The only source of illumination was a portable, battery-powered light in the corner. At first, the man from the Housing Authority could not make out the other man's face, but he knew it was the same man. He sensed it. The man held a long piece of black metal in each of his hands. Behind the hands, a large knife was sheathed and tucked into the front of the man's pants. The stranger stopped whistling and took three slow steps forward, removing his face from the darkness. Not only did Abdella know this place, he knew this man. It was the same man from the road, but now the mustache and long hair under the baseball cap were missing. The prisoner searched his memory for the man standing before him. His captor spoke two words that told Abdella where he was, and why. It only took a few seconds for him to realize who the man was and what would come next.

Now, Abdella knew *exactly* what he had done to deserve this.

Mayton had thought about this moment for over a year. He thought about what he would say to Abdella when the time came. From the look on Abdella's face, nothing needed to be said. The man this city celebrated as an American success story understood now. He knew he was going to die. The only thing he did not know was what Mayton was going to do to him after he killed him. Mayton took five more steps toward Abdella, leaned down, and quietly told him. He told him everything. He told him how he was going to kill him and the disgrace that would follow. When Mayton stopped speaking, it was then, and only then, that Abdella started screaming. Mayton did not try to silence his victim. Nobody would hear him. He had faith. It was God's will.

STEP 4

We made a searching and fearless moral inventory of ourselves.

Channing and Lambert spent the rest of the evening tracking down and interviewing various city council members, none of whom was particularly helpful. Each council member was eager to express condemnation of the murder of Nicholas Culligan and affirm the city's government would stand together in the aftermath of this horrible attack on one of their own. Each member was also quick to state that they did not know Culligan well, and while they could not imagine anyone wanting to harm him, they were oddly adamant that they knew nothing of his personal dealings or non-council-related activities. By the time the detectives finished, they had the impression that the murdered councilman would not be missed by his colleagues, regardless of what was said when cameras and microphones were present.

By ten o'clock that same night, Channing and Lambert sat in a dimly lit conference room at the station, eating Chinese take-out while watching the video recordings from the parking garage and the areas around the Clemente Bridge. Although they had put in a full day's work, the hollow sentiments conveyed by the council members left the investigators with a void they needed to fill. They needed a lead. Any lead.

First, they watched the recording from the entrance of the parking garage. It did not take long to find the portion of the recording where Culligan had driven into the structure. From there, they decided to start their review from one hour prior to his arrival to one hour after. They were operating on the assumption that whoever killed Culligan would not want to wait too long in the garage, out of fear of being noticed. Another assumption they had to make was that, if the killer drove Culligan's body out of the garage, he or she would not sit around for too long after the killing, especially considering the noticeable amount of blood around the councilman's car.

They watched the garage video together several times. Dozens of cars entered the garage during the timeframe they had designated. Even though the camera was perched at such a high angle that passengers were not visible and license plates could not be seen, the detectives did their best to jot down the makes and models of each of the vehicles. On two occasions, Channing tried to make conversation with Lambert. On two occasions all he got back was an icy, "Uh huh."

It was after midnight when they moved on to the recordings from the south side of the bridge. The image quality was exactly what one would expect from an old rental car company. Not surprisingly, the camera angle had been adjusted to keep watch over the inventory of cars, but at the top of their monitor, the detectives could see some traffic moving along Sixth Street. Lambert fast-forwarded the recording to 8:30 p.m. The detectives had discussed the timeline and decided that since the first call about Culligan's body was a 9:03 p.m., going back about thirty minutes on the recording would be logical. They doubted a body could dangle off the bridge for more than a few minutes before someone noticed, so whatever vehicle transported the body would have mostly likely passed through the area just prior to and after the first call to 9-1-1.

Repeating the process of viewing the garage video, Lambert and Channing started taking note of what vehicles passed by on the monitor. Not knowing which direction the killer had driven from before depositing the body, the detectives had to account for vehicles driving both north and south. Much like the garage video, the angle of the camera only allowed for general observations and did not reveal license plate numbers or any views of inside the cars. Lambert let the recording run until the time stamp hit 9:15 p.m., then stood and hit the stop button.

Arching her back in a prolonged stretch, Lambert glanced at a clock on the wall as she asked, "Want to check our notes against the garage video now or do it all after we look at the recordings from the north side of the bridge?"

When no reply came, she turned, expecting to see Channing, but was surprised to only find a rotating desk chair. She looked across the squad room and caught a glimpse of the senior detective's back as he quickly walked to the men's room. At each end of the chair's black armrests, Lambert could discern fading hand prints left over from Channing's perspiration.

Channing received a glare from his partner when he returned to the conference room. His cheeks looked flushed.

Meekly, he said, "You made the right call with the Hunan tofu. The General Tso's chicken isn't quite right."

Lambert's expression left no mistake that she was less than impressed with her new partner. The judgment she wordlessly conveyed made Channing wonder if everyone viewed him similarly. How far had he fallen in the eyes of his compatriots? If they were all using the same mathematics that he was when trying to assess himself, then the equation was simple: *Jackson Channing* ≤ 0.

Channing made a pathetic, but ultimately successful attempt to change the unspoken subject.

"Do you think we should check our notes against the parking garage video now or wait until we look at the other tape?"

Lambert waited a few ticks before responding with an obviously condescending grin.

"I just asked you the same question, but General Tso interrupted us."

The former All-American runner broke eye contact and stretched by swiveling her torso back and forth. She had obviously stayed in shape since her days competing at Duquesne University, where at one time or another she had run every event from the sixteen hundred meter to the three thousand meter. By her senior year, she had even participated in the Olympic Trials at the longer of the distances, but quickly discovered that she had reached her potential and any Olympic dreams were unrealistic.

She finished her stretching. "Let's look at the last video and then start cross-referencing vehicles."

Channing nodded. He felt sick again, but this time it was simply an overwhelming feeling of depression associated with discovering how weak he had become. He wondered if he had ever been empathetic to others who felt like this—those that had addictions; the ones haunted by demons they could see, but not fully understand. Was this some sort of karma? A reckoning for his sins?

"…recordings."

Channing's head snapped up. He had mentally checked out again.

"I'm sorry. What?" he asked.

"You asked if we should look at the last tape. They don't use video tapes anymore. Everything is digital and then burned to disc. They are just recordings. I just don't want you to write down the word tapes in any of your notes or reports. When this goes to trial, the attorneys are going to pick everything apart."

"Right," Channing said. "You're absolutely right. Let's look at the last recording."

– – –

The work on Abdella was complete. *Luke 6:36* had always instructed Mayton to be merciful, so he was not. It was all very confusing to the man who had once wanted to join the clergy, but found he did not have the charisma needed to sway audiences. That, and owning an unpleasant voice that seemed to screech when he attempted to speak loudly, made any thoughts of addressing a congregation unbearable.

To do the Lord's work he had to act contrary to the Lord's word. Did that make him similar to one of the zealots who selectively chose passages from the Bible or the Quran and then blew up buildings and harmed children? He did not know how to reconcile the contradictions in his life; he only knew that somehow the scales had to balance. A life had been taken and her life had been worth all of theirs put together. Whether the words were, "Do unto others" or, if one preferred the Old Testament, "An eye for an eye", the same message was conveyed: balance. Some Eastern religions counted on karma to maintain life's equilibrium, even if it depended on the existence of a future life. Mayton had to admit one of his biggest flaws had always been a lack of patience. He needed to see justice done in *this* lifetime.

"I don't think you're going to get many visitors in here today, Lester."

The old man's voice startled Mayton. He dropped the items in his hands and they clanked together next to his feet.

"It's chillier out there than my first wife's reaction when I told her I was lookin' forward to shipping out to Korea because the cookin' was better and the chances of her mother visiting me were pretty slim!"

Rick laughed at his own joke and Mayton, who was sitting on a barrel next to the fire, made a sad attempt to show amusement.

Rick took a few steps inside the cabin and let the door close behind him.

"You okay there, buddy? You're looking a little green around the gills. You're not coming down with something are you?"

"No. Just tired I guess."

"Thinkin' about that wife of yours? I only met her a couple of times, but she sure was a sweet thing."

Mayton did not want to have this conversation. Who was this man to presume that he knew Cindy at all? Who was he to assume that he knew what was on Mayton's mind? How could he have the nerve to—?

"Look, Lester. I've been married three times. I lost the

first wife to my own stupidity and my second to a heart attack."

Rick took another step toward his audience of one, looking around at all the items on the walls, when Mayton kicked some straw that was on the floor over the items he had dropped.

"Life goes on, my friend. I lost a lot of friends in Korea and Father Time took most of the rest. All you can do is appreciate what time you have and make the most of it. You have to overcome adversity when it stares you in the face. What was it Martin Luther King said? 'A man is judged by how he handles challenges.' Well, I think that's how we figure out who we really are."

Mayton knew the quote Rick was referring to and recited it in his head. *The ultimate measure of a man is not where he stands in moments of comfort and convenience, but where he stands at times of challenge and controversy.*

Lester was just staring into the fire. The old man had stopped his approach; there was something in Mayton's eyes. Modern soldiers would have probably called it the *thousand yard stare.* Rick was not sure what to call it, but he took it as an invitation to leave.

"Well...I...uh, I'm going to go take care of them horses. They don't much like the cold either. You take care, Lester."

Just as he had not heard the door open, he did not hear Rick close the door on his way out. Mayton kept gazing into the fire and snapped out of his trance only when he smelled the straw at his feet starting to burn. Quickly, he stamped out the smoldering straw and picked up the instruments he had dropped.

The measure of a man. In the past, Mayton would say it was not his place to measure or assess the acts of others. That time was gone. Mayton returned his attention to his instruments. They had to be perfect. He worked on them for the better part of an hour, looking over every detail. He measured the first one. Then he measured the second, which would be identical to the first. The third was already hanging on the wall exactly where Rick had been looking.

— — —

"I'm not authorizing the BOLO."

Harris was adamant and his tone did not leave the impression that his mind could be changed, but Lambert tried anyway.

"It's the only lead we've got! What's the harm in putting it out there? If you aren't going to issue the lookout for law enforcement, let's at least give it to the press!"

"No way," was the sergeant's only reply.

"And why the hell not?"

Harris raised his eyebrows and gave Channing a look that said, *You explain it to her.*

Channing turned toward his partner. "Remember the D.C. sniper investigation a few years ago?"

"What about it?"

"They had a witness who said they saw a white van driving away from one of the shootings. The next thing you know, hundreds of cops spent countless hours looking for a suspect in white van. In fact, the case was so jacked up from the onset, the FBI profile of the shooter was just as inaccurate as the vehicle description. Everyone down there was looking for a white male, loner type in a white van, while two black guys were cruising around in a dark Chevy Caprice picking people off at will."

Lambert was not giving up and Channing understood why. He had been down that road before. When you only have one thread of evidence, you pull on that thread until something unravels or it breaks off in your hand. However, in this case, Channing knew Harris was right.

"We have to put it out there! A white van was seen leaving the parking garage right after Culligan's time of death. Then, a similar van was seen heading onto the Clemente Bridge from the south and exiting to the north, but only after a longer-than-expected delay. It's got to be the suspect's vehicle."

Channing looked back at Harris, who was stoically staring at the coffee mug on his desk again. Channing thought, *That has got to be the most fascinating damn mug in the history of law enforcement.* Channing cleared his throat in an attempt to break the spell of the hypnotic mug.

Harris looked up and said, "We can't risk a repeat of what happened in D.C. If we put vague information like this out, with no license plate number or driver description, we're asking for trouble. We need more before we put the info out there."

Channing had tried to explain all this to Lambert before they went to see their sergeant. However, as soon as Channing had started to give his opinion, she had cut him off and insisted on taking the matter to Harris. Now that Harris had confirmed what Channing had started to say, the youngest of the investigators was incensed.

"Then at least give me a new partner."

Now it was Channing's turn to look at the coffee mug.

Harris stood up. "We've covered this already and that issue is closed."

Now Channing had confirmation that he was the subject of the first animated conversation he had witnessed between his two coworkers. The angry silhouette pacing on the other side of Malloy's door had been imploring him to give her a partner who did not come with so much baggage.

"You two get back out there and find some of Culligan's enemies. Somebody thought this out enough that they climbed under a fucking bridge in the middle of a city and rigged ropes so they would support a body. Not an easy task without some serious equipment, mind you. Not to mention, the killer treated a city councilman like a voodoo doll and nearly cut his head off." Harris took an overdue breath. "Did the forensics report come back yet?"

Channing let Lambert answer. Better to let her get her mind back on the task at hand. Besides, she was the lead detective and had to feel like she just got double-teamed by the good ole boys club.

"The cause of death was the gash across his throat. The M.E. said that if his throat wouldn't have been cut, he would have died soon enough anyway. Both lungs were punctured by something sharp and round. Not like a knife, but round like a big nail." Lambert looked down and referred to the forensics report she had in her hand, flipped a page, read a few lines, and looked back up. "The initial tox screen was negative and there were no signs of any other trauma, other than some bruising on Culligan's back that appears to be at the same height as the roof of his Lexus. I'm figuring that he was stabbed with this thing and fell back against his car before he got his throat cut.

"Also, about the throat…. The M.E. said the cut was deep, but wasn't made by the sharpest blade. Something with a smooth edge—not serrated like a lot of knives are. So whoever did this had some serious upper-body strength."

Harris nodded and asked, "Anything else?"

Lambert seemed to hesitate and then, after some internal debate, came to a conclusion. "There was some dark transfer of material around the wounds on the victim's chest and neck. Some of it is on his shirt where the punctures were made, too. The lab results are going to take a couple more days." Lambert stood a little taller, put both hands behind her back, and looked at the wall in front of her. "It would have been visible at the scene."

There it was. That was what she had been holding back from Channing when he recounted his observations at the scene. He had made the conclusion that Culligan had been shot and Lambert knew that if Channing had done his job worth a damn, he would have noticed the dark marks around the wounds and either looked at the wounds more closely or mentioned that it appeared gunshot residue was on the shirt. If he missed the residue around the neck, that could be easily explained by the substantial amount of blood that had poured out of the cut. Channing took a deep breath and realized Lambert recognized his incompetence from the very start. Not only was his reputation damaged from previous events, but he was building himself an entirely different type of bad reputation due to his shoddy performance at the scene. At that moment, he wanted nothing more than to get out of that office and head into a bathroom stall. The flask was calling his name.

Harris knew what all of this meant and managed to keep his facial expression neutral. He nodded and tried not to allow any awkward pauses to enter into his office.

"These are very specific facts. Check the files for any crimes we've had where similar weapons may have been used—a knife that left a trace and some other weapon that created a puncture wound in somebody."

It was the sergeant's use of the singular *wound* that steered Channing's thoughts away from the flask that was so very close to him.

"Wounds," he said as if responding to a conversation that only he could hear.

"What?" asked Harris.

"Wounds—plural." Channing looked up from the mug. "I think we're looking for three weapons, not two."

Harris and Lambert waited.

"The punctures in Culligan's chest came first, right?"

The other two investigators agreed.

"Well, let's say you get stabbed in one side of the chest and pinned against a car..."

Channing quickly took hold of Lambert's shoulder, turned her toward him and made a stabbing motion with his right hand.

"What is your reaction going to be?"

Lambert, still trying to comprehend the fact she was being stabbed by a mentally unstable detective holding an imaginary weapon in his hand, said, "I'm going to reach out and try to grab the weapon that's in my chest."

The female detective reached up with both hands toward Channing's fist, which was balled up just above her left breast.

"And look what you did." He smiled and paused to give Harris and Lambert a chance to process what was happening. "You instinctively reached up with both hands and pulled your right arm across your chest..."

Lambert's eyes opened a little wider and she understood.

She finished his sentence with, "Covering the area where the other puncture wound was inflicted."

Channing continued his demonstration and had his

partner lower her arms again.

"And there were no other wounds to suggest there was much of a struggle. So, the stab wounds would most likely be simultaneous." With that, he raised both his hands and violently plunged both fists in a stabbing motion toward his partner's chest, stopping just short of actually hitting her with force. "Which means he was either using one very large, symmetrical weapon with two sharp rounded points—not the easiest thing to conceal or maneuver in close quarters—or he had two weapons, one in each hand." With that, Channing proceeded to repeat the double-stabbing motion, but this time pushed Lambert all the way against a wall.

"I stab the victim, puncture both lungs—taking the fight out of him—which gives me all kinds of time to reach for a knife and…"

Channing pulled a pen out of his jacket pocket and slashed it across Lambert's neck. She was surprised to find that the look in his eyes and his sudden animation during the entire demonstration both scared and excited her. She could feel her heart beating in her chest. It was not sexual excitement; it was the type of excitement one experiences with an adrenaline rush. Only she felt like her rush was a vicarious one. She could feel *his* excitement. *His* passion. Where in the hell did that come from?

Channing finished his pen-assisted coup de grâce, felt a sudden influx of embarrassment, then put the pen back in his jacket pocket.

Looking away from Lambert, he said, "Uh…so…I'm thinking Culligan was killed with three weapons. Two were used simultaneously, and then the knife a few seconds later."

The room was quiet for a moment, and then Harris broke the silence.

"Okay. So go check on any potentially related cases and start tracking down anyone who held a grudge against Culligan." Looking at Lambert, he added, "Keep the white van thing in mind. You may be one-hundred-percent right on the vehicle. We just need more information before we act on it."

– – –

She took Mayton's hand as they walked through the woods. There was a light coating of snow on the path and they could hear the gentle crunching of the flakes with every step. He loved these walks. Listening to her talk and seeing her warm breath stream through the chilled air was the most peaceful experience he could imagine. She was telling him that she wanted for them to go on a trip together, a vacation to Aruba or maybe the Dominican Republic. She wanted to see different things and wanted him to try to relax more. He smiled and indulged her, but he knew he would not spend the money on something as wasteful as a vacation. Too many other obligations required his attention.

His mind must have drifted as they walked because now they were in their bedroom. Cindy was pacing and he was sitting on the bed. It was their bed, but the room was somehow different. The walls seemed darker and the overhead light fixture gave off a yellow hue.

She was upset—angry even. An envelope holding airline tickets was in her hand.

She was mad at him and he was just saying, "No. There are more important things to do than travel."

She was crying now, but rather than comfort her, he pushed harder.

"Why don't we just pray on it? Pray with me, darling. Pray with me."

She would not even look at him. She stared at a painting hanging in the room. A painting he did not recognize.

"Pray with me, Cindy. Pray with me."

She turned toward him, started to speak, then reached up and started pulling her hair out. She cried harder. The hair came out in giant fistfuls. In her hands, her brown hair looked gray and she had it interwoven between her fingers. Her head was now bald with the exception of a few bloody patches of hair. She dropped to her knees. He reached out for her, but she slapped his hand away. Then, she screamed so loudly he had to cover his ears, and when he raised his hands to block out the noise, they were full of her hair. Then, he could taste it in his mouth. He opened his mouth and could feel the long strands hanging over his lips. He was choking on a large ball of hair that filled his mouth and throat. He could not breathe.

He could not...

He hardly ever dreamed. Well, that was not true. Mayton was sure he dreamed, but he was not one of those people who could usually remember dreams after he awoke. When he opened his eyes, it took him a few seconds to realize he was in his own bed. Then, his heart leapt and he turned to his left where Cindy used to slumber. The emptiness in the bed did not compare to the cavernous ache he felt when he realized that it had just been a dream. She was still gone. He had still failed her. He still had work to do.

Mayton looked at the clock, which read 4:30 a.m. Knowing that falling asleep again would be impossible, he decided to get an early start on his morning workout. A year ago, he was a slight man, but now his arms and shoulders bulged out of his shirt. Before Cindy died, he rarely exercised, but once he had plotted a course of action, he began shaping his body in the same manner he shaped all his instruments. His torso was now solid, fully functional, and, when necessary, lethal. Getting under the Clemente Bridge had been easy. He found it amazing how—if you wore a reflective yellow vest, put on a hardhat, and set a few orange traffic cones around an area—nobody seemed to question your reason for being there. Do it early on a Monday morning, before the commuters start roaming around, and people are just happy that work is being done before rush hour starts.

From his boat, Mayton had surveyed the bottom of the bridge. He did not want to draw any attention by sitting below the bridge taking photographs, so he had simply passed under the bright yellow structure several times in the previous weeks and then sketched the underside by memory. Once he had the details of the bridge drawn out, he calculated exactly where ropes would have to be tied in order for him to: first, get the rope in place that would hold Culligan's body; and second, allow Mayton to quickly reach under the walkway, retrieve the rope, and then tie the body onto it and drop Culligan over the side of the bridge.

Mayton had gone to the library to purchase all the necessary equipment online. He had everything shipped to his church, telling the lady in the church's main office that he was rarely home to sign for packages. The woman, understanding the recent widower was still adjusting to living alone, never questioned him about the boxes that were delivered.

The hardhat, vest, cones, and pulley had been easy enough to find. Within a few days, he was ready to go to work. The entire setup had gone off without a hitch. The only oversight he made was not buying gloves good enough to protect his hands from abrasive ropes, of which he had an abundant supply. Using his newly acquired upper-body strength, he was able to set up his simple system of ropes in about twenty minutes.

There had been a brief scare when Mayton picked up his cones to walk back to his van, which waited near the baseball stadium. A police officer slowed down on the bridge, unrolled his window, and asked Mayton if he was getting hazardous duty pay for "doing that shit". Mayton, doing his best to mask his social awkwardness, managed to force himself to give a general *working man's* reply and even forced himself to toss in a profanity for good measure. He figured he must have done it right, because the cop gave a chuckle and drove on.

It would be another twenty-four hours or so before he would act again. Surely, Abdella's wife would have reported him missing by now. As far as Culligan was concerned, the police would be focusing on his endless supply of enemies or trying to identify anyone who would gain from his death. While the police could possibly get around to talking to Mayton eventually, he still had plenty of time. It was almost funny now. When he first started to think about doing all of this, he was not sure he had it in him. Now, his doubts were few and his will was stronger than ever. Culligan was just the opening line of his message—a nice little attention getter. Tomorrow, he would start to compose the main body.

STEP 5

We admitted to God, to ourselves, and to another human being the exact nature of our wrongs.

Of all the things to get to him, it was a damn song. Not long after midnight, Channing was driving home from the station, all of his mental faculties fully engaged with the murder of Councilman Culligan, when he turned on the car stereo. He did not know why, but sometimes music helped him think. He supposed it stimulated some creative part of his mind and allowed him to think outside the box. Or, maybe the melodies occupied a part of his mind that tended to focus too hard on a case, causing him to over-analyze rather than simplify. Whatever the reasoning, clicking on the stereo usually helped.

He was a few blocks from his modest home on Pittsburgh's South Side when the song playing on the radio caught his attention. That song, *Wicked Game*, had been playing when he first danced with Mary. They had just met a few days earlier when Channing was standing in line at a park, waiting to register for a local 5K race. Mary was sitting at a table writing names down and handing runners their assigned racing bibs and T-shirts labeled with the name of the race. She was beautiful, but not in the superficial Cosmo magazine sense of the word. She simply glowed and he was immediately attracted to her.

When he got to the front of the line, she asked for his name, date of birth—so he could be put in the proper age grouping—and his phone number.

He replied, "Jackson Channing. And today must be my birthday because you just asked for my phone number."

She looked up from her clipboard, smiled at him, really seeing him for the first time, and said, "I'll just mark you down for the *Under 10* age group, and you should probably give me your mommy's phone number in case you fall down and get a boo-boo."

Taking the not-so-subtle hint, he grabbed his race packet and headed off toward the starting area. It was not until the next day, when he checked the race website to see the results, that he realized his name was not listed in his proper age group. Rolling his eyes, he checked the *Under 10* division and still could not find his name. He scrolled through the results for another two minutes before he saw that one group stood alone at the bottom of the page. It was listed as the *Socially Impaired, but Cute* division and had one name under it. The smile that spanned across his face was broader than any bridge in the city. It took only one phone call to the race organizer to get Mary's email address. By that same evening, they had a date planned for the weekend.

The restaurant was in the North Shore neighborhood of the city, known for its abundance of great Italian food and shortage of adequate parking. The pair met there at eight o'clock, and by ten had retreated to the bar in the rear. By eleven, it was obvious to both of them that they were a great match. She took his hand and led him to the dance floor the minute the first slow song played. It was *that* song. That damn song. They danced incredibly slow and kissed incredibly long.

That song.

He didn't even bother taking his coat off. Once he hit the front door, he went straight to the kitchen where he had half a bottle of Jack Daniels above the sink. At first, he mixed it with Coke. Then he ran out of Coke. Then he ran out of Jack. He rummaged around the house and found a six-pack of beer in his pantry. It was not cold, but he did not care. He sat on his couch in his—their—darkened living room, sipping warm beer and thinking of her.

He blamed her at first. In the weeks and months after he was found in that damp, begrimed basement, he blamed her for his shortcomings. *She* did not understand him. *She* was not supportive enough. *She* was pushing him to get back to work too quickly. *She, she, she.* He continued to disconnect from her, and she reciprocated. Rather than acknowledge the damage he was inflicting, he created a hazy version of reality, clouded by alcohol and painkillers. When the doctors stopped giving him enough pills, he drank more alcohol. Then one evening, they were arguing about something he could barely remember. Maybe it was his drinking, or the fact that he had not left the house in weeks. Regardless, he snapped. He did not physically hurt her, but he said something terrible, then grabbed and shook her. It was then that she looked in his eyes and did not recognize the man she had loved. This stranger was full and empty all at the same time. Full of rage, hatred, regret, and bitterness. Empty of a soul. She left when he passed out. Gone.

Channing knew the drinking was not helping. But when he

heard that song, the thirst he experienced was something he had no defense against. On more than one occasion, he had halfheartedly tried to build a dam of sobriety, and each time it was washed over by the flood of quenching fluid he now poured down his throat. How could it dominate his mind and body like this? How could it develop into such a compulsion that logic and reason—his cornerstones—no longer mattered? He leaned back on the couch and became drowsy. The bottle of beer he was holding slid out of his hand and dropped to the floor, spilling a portion of its contents onto the carpet.

Channing couldn't remember the last time he prayed. Maybe it was in that basement. He did not know if he believed in God, but he wanted to. Did he have to say the words aloud? He did not think so. He looked up at the ceiling. *God*, he thought. *It wasn't her fault. It was mine.*

Waking up enough to find the cell phone in his pocket, he hit the speed dial option for her cell phone—like he had done countless times in the past few weeks—and like before, the phone rang four times and then went to voice mail. Always four times.

After supplying the voice mail with a few seconds of dead air, he managed to slur, "It was me. I'm sorry."

He searched for and found the *end call* button on his phone and pushed it. He put the phone on the end table beside him, and searched for the bottle that lay somewhere around his feet.

— — —

The new tarp in the back of the van had a strong plastic odor to it, but it was not nearly enough to cover up the stench beginning to emanate from Abdella's body. Mayton kept telling himself that suffering was part of the deal. He did not dare open any of the windows as he drove through the city, as a passerby—if there were any this time of night— might notice the foulness coming from the vehicle. *Just a few more minutes*, he kept telling himself.

Driving up the winding roads to Mt. Washington, he found himself thinking of Moses ascending Mt. Sinai, only to later climb down bearing the Ten Commandments: those uncomplicated laws created by a God who had tried to simplify things as much as possible for a pathetic race of creatures who think they can make up their own rules.

A smirk came across Mayton's face and he thought, *Stone tablets won't do the job in this day and age.* Mayton knew he would have to break some of the sacred rules to chisel his actions into the stone psyches of others.

He pressed down harder on the accelerator as the van struggled up the side of the hill overlooking the city. Mt. Washington was primarily known for its restaurants with scenic views of the Pittsburgh skyline and for the Duquesne Incline, which was essentially a trolley car that ran up and down the hill on rails and cables. Serving as more of a tourist attraction than a real form of transit, it transported passengers between the base of the hill near downtown and the top. Mayton always considered it to be an overrated tourist trap, but regardless of his dislike for the Incline, it was visible to much of the city, so it had become a symbol unique to Pittsburgh.

The thoughts of Moses and all he endured led Mayton's mind into the theological realm he tried to avoid. What did it take to make people listen? When does an outcast become a respected leader, and when will corrupt leaders be recognized as the oppressors? Mayton had tried to lead the way. He had tried to steer others toward God. He had tried to lead Cindy along the path of righteousness. Not only did he lead her by example, but also by his words.

She had been much younger than he, but that had not mattered. Her beauty was breathtaking, but that had not been what had drawn him to her. It was her voice. She sang like an angel and he could pick her voice out of the entire church choir. He had never been able to do that before—isolate a voice in the group. As was his custom, he had been sitting in the front pew and when the choir started singing, he instantly detected something different. Something he had never heard in all the years he had been in the congregation. When he scanned the choir in an attempt to find the aberration, he focused in on her. After the service, he approached the choir director to ask who the owner of the talented voice was.

Her name was Cindy Eaton and she had just moved to the area so she could finish her graduate work at Chatham University. She was in her early twenties and was classmates with another member of the choir, Leslie Stewart. Leslie had talked Cindy, who was a bit shy, into coming to church with her and eventually convinced her to join the choir. Mayton, who always arrived early, had never noticed the shy newcomer hiding in the back pew. He certainly noticed her now.

When she said *yes* to having dinner with him that first time, he got the impression that she did so more out of politeness than an actual desire to get to know him better. But before long, he had won her over with his kind disposition and subdued demeanor. He loved her bashfulness and she loved listening to him go on and on about history, philosophy, and theology. Back then, Mayton did not shy away from discussing the works of pre-Christian scholars and the heathens who had yet to be saved. It was not until later that he decided such intellectual pursuits were a waste of time not worthy of conversation.

Their wedding had been a simple affair held in their church. Cindy wore a classic dress and Mayton a plain black suit. If one compared the wedding photos of the two to those of newly married couples taken a hundred years prior, there would be few differences. This was the way Mayton wanted things. Traditions became traditional because they worked in society and led to balance in the home.

Something changed in Cindy after the first few years of marriage. Wanting to have a job, when he could provide adequately for both of them, was just one of the things that he struggled to comprehend. That book club she joined did not help matters one bit. The so-called *literary works* they read and openly discussed sickened him. The vivid descriptions of gratuitous sex and violence were symptoms of the disease infecting society, and here she was not only reading that smut, but openly talking about it as if further analysis was even warranted.

The van reached the top of the hill and he stopped at the traffic signal. He flipped on the turn signal and waited. A low rattle reverberated through the van as the engine idled. He could have made the right on red, but he just sat there on the abandoned street, deep in thought while the turn signal made a low clicking noise.

The clock in the marriage counselor's office clicked like that: rhythmic and judgmental; precise and surgical. She insisted they try counseling as a way to communicate better. She said she did not feel as if he was listening to her. Cindy claimed that whenever they argued, he would simply quote pieces of scripture or put a religious spin on the topic and then make a final proclamation that the subject was closed. She was right. Mayton's father had been like that, but his mother had known her place. She was a quiet woman like Cindy was when Mayton first met her. Throughout Mayton's life, his mother had always deferred to his father on any major decision making.

That's the way it's supposed to be, thought Mayton. *That was her role and she played it well. Even Plato—a pagan—defined true justice as occurring when people fulfilled the role that was intended for them.*

The marriage counselor immediately took Cindy's side. Every time Mayton mentioned the Bible, the smarmy little man dismissed his comments—dismissed them! When Mayton warned the man that he was in danger of going to Hell, the man cockily leaned back in his fancy leather chair and seemed to pronounce a silent judgment on Mayton. All the time that man sat there surgically dissecting Mayton's performance as a husband and provider, that clock's ticking grew louder and louder. How dare he judge!

Mayton tried to imagine what his father would have done if his mother tried to drag him to some godless shrink. To his knowledge, Mayton's mother never attempted any such lunacy. She kept a good home and took care of her family.

Mayton stared at the his hands on the hard steering wheel and envisioned his mother waving to him as the school bus pulled away.

She was satisfied with her station in life, wasn't she?

At the end of her life, long after his father had gone to the Lord, she did seem to talk more and more about what she called her *unbroken piggy bank of dreams.* Mayton never asked her what that meant. Maybe he did not want to know. In the final days, his mother—whose ramblings had become borderline unintelligible—cried a lot. She said the tears were not for the approaching end of her life, but the life she never knew. She mumbled random words like *dancing, travel,* and most curiously, *dry martinis.* In all his life, Mayton had never seen his mother partake in alcohol, so he assumed her words were simply the final warning signs before her passing. Now he wondered. Had his mother really been happy? Did she have dreams left untouched? On her journey to the afterlife, was the one thing she held on to not a lifetime of wonderful memories, but a collection of regrets?

Cindy often talked about not wanting to *miss out* on anything. She said they were still young, and since they did not seem capable of having children, they should devote some of their time and money to seeing the world and experiencing new things.

Did Cindy have an unbroken piggy bank, too?

Was she right?

Did he listen to her enough?

Did he listen at all?

Mayton felt his eyes tear up. Is that how she came to see him, as…an obstacle? Had he become an obstruction to her happiness instead of her loving partner? As she wasted away in that bed, her fair skin shrinking away, revealing her frail bones, what was she really thinking? He thought her stoicism was due to the fear of death, but now he had doubts. Was it actually…regret?

My God, he thought, *I was a **regret** to her.*

With that, something broke inside of him and the tears flowed freely. His heart raced and his breathing became rapid. At first, he thought he might be having a heart attack, but he forced himself to take a few deep breaths and everything started to slow down. He counted backwards from ten and tried to calm himself. He heard no sound, except for the clicking of the turn signal, then a loud horn blast made him jump. There was a car behind him waiting to turn. Mayton did not know how long he had been at the light, but he was certain he had sat through several cycles.

Making the right turn onto Grandview Avenue, he pulled the van over to the side of the road, wiped his eyes, and looked out over the city. He had work to do and the timing was critical, but his new revelations concerning his faults were too much. He dug around in the glove box and found his gold crucifix, then he prayed for several minutes. He could not keep the guilt of what he had become to Cindy to himself. He had to talk to someone. From the van's unused ashtray, he pulled out a cell phone. It was nearly four o'clock in the morning, but this could not wait. He punched in the number and breathed a sigh of relief when the groggy-sounding man answered.

– – –

Channing opened his eyes and could make out the stomp texture on the ceiling. His head was leaning on the back of the couch, while his body was still mostly in a sitting position. He did not know how long he had been out, but from the dryness of his mouth—which must have been wide open—it had been a while. Slowly, he straightened his neck, feeling the tiny muscles struggle to function as he blinked and tried to figure out what had disturbed his sleep.

He was hammered. He knew the experience well, and knew better than to move too quickly. The amount of alcohol in his system was not enormous by his standards, but on an empty stomach, it had done the trick. Channing rubbed his eyes and rolled his neck. A tapping noise was coming from…somewhere. He made a feeble attempt to stand, and steadied himself on the second attempt.

An empty beer bottle spun across the room as Channing accidentally kicked it when attempting to take a step around the coffee table. The noise, which was a little louder now, came from his left. Walking toward the front door, he finally recognized it as knocking. Half walking, half shuffling in that direction, he opened the door without checking who was on the other side. Illuminated by a yellow porch light, Tina Lambert looked alert and confident. As she sized up the form standing in the doorway, her expression changed to frustration, but just as quickly—concern.

"Sorry to bother you so late."

Channing did not speak. He simply left the door open, walked back to the couch, and sat down. He made no effort to hide the empty bottles surrounding him. Lambert stood in the doorway, unsure if she should leave or if the open door was Channing's idea of an invitation. He was obviously drunk and he had to realize she would be able to tell. So, if walking away from the open door was an invitation, it was one filled with indifference.

"What time is it?" Channing inquired as he sorted through beer bottles, trying to find one that still contained fluid.

"It's nearly three o'clock," answered Lambert. "I couldn't sleep, took a drive. I thought you might be up, so I called dispatch and got your address. I drove up, saw your light on and…well, here I am."

Channing found a bottle that was not quite empty and drained it into his mouth. He lowered the bottle and his eyes dropped to a space on the floor between his feet.

Lambert waited for him to speak, but after twenty

seconds, it became apparent that the ball was in her court.

"I hope you don't mind. I just thought we could talk and maybe clear up some things."

Her partner's head didn't move, but Lambert could tell his eyes were still open. This time she used the silence to look around the living room. Modest and tasteful furniture. It looked to be a recently neglected home, littered with empty bottles. Pictures of Channing and the woman who must be, or once was, his wife decorated walls and tables. Some medals were hanging from a set of pegs on the wall.

As a former star high school and collegiate athlete, she knew the kind of display. She had a similar set-up displaying some of her achievements on the track. She was only a few years removed from putting on dominating displays of speed, but now it seemed so long ago. So many miles, so many victories, so many athletic and academic accolades and here she was: a cop, staring at her alcoholic partner at three in the morning, working a grisly homicide, and fighting for respect from both the public and her own department.

She looked over at the top of Channing's head, breathed in air thick with the smell of alcohol, and shook her head while wondering what her mother would say about this. The woman who had given her so much, while having so little. The woman who cleaned houses and wiped the noses of children that did not belong to her in order to give her own daughter a chance at a better life. The woman who died happy, knowing her only child was going to go to college to become a doctor, or a lawyer, or…something other than this.

"Look," Lambert said in her most maternal tone. "I don't know all the details about what happened to you, but I know what I saw from you today in Harris's office. You were energized. You were…sharp. You were—"

"Relatively sober." Channing interrupted and looked over at a picture of him and his wife. They were standing in front of a fountain at a local park. Channing remembered handing his cell phone to some random woman and asking her to take the picture. What was it—two, maybe three years ago?

Lambert let the silence settle back in and immediately regretted it. Now she would have to fill the void again.

"I just wanted to tell you that I'm sorry if I came across as icy. I can do that sometimes. It's a defense mechanism and I need to work on it. It's nothing personal. If half of the rumors about you are true, it's amazing that you even came back to work."

She paused, not sure she wanted to say the next thing on her mind.

Keeping a calm tone, she suggested, "I'm sure you could change your mind and still take some sort of early retirement, or a light duty assignment, or something like that."

If Channing was listening, he did not let it show. He was still looking at the picture on the other side of the room.

Another few seconds passed and Lambert decided she should leave. She pulled her keys out of her pocket and turned toward the door.

The metallic sound of the keys banging together seemed to register with Channing. He spoke in a quiet and serious tone.

"I was working the Drifter case. It was really just mop-up duty at that point. Making sure we had all our ducks in a row for court. No heavy lifting. Just doing everything we could to make sure he didn't walk on a technicality."

Lambert stopped and turned around. At first, she thought he was talking some sort of drunken nonsense. Then, she replayed the words in her mind—Drifter case—and she knew where her partner was going with this, but she was not sure it was a good thing.

Stanley Drifter had abducted, raped, and killed three gay men in the area. He tripped up when he tried to grab what would have been victim number four behind a bar that was a favorite of Pittsburgh's homosexual community, not realizing that his slight-looking target had a black belt in judo. A beaten and battered Drifter escaped with a broken arm and multiple cuts and scrapes. Through witness descriptions and a canvas of the local hospitals, Channing and his partner, Alex Belmont, tracked Drifter down and subsequently discovered a treasure chest of physical evidence in his home. As far as murder cases went, it was pretty much open-and-shut.

Channing leaned his head back on the couch and closed his eyes. "We were just following up with Drifter's neighbors—asking the usual questions: Did you see anything unusual at Drifter's house? Did you ever have any problems with him? Ever notice a lot of vehicles coming and going? Basically, checking to see if there might be any more victims that we didn't know about. Nothing unusual."

Lambert uncomfortably played with the keys in her hands and wondered if her visit was a big mistake.

"We'd probably hit six or seven houses on the street and hadn't come up with anything new. Everybody said the same thing. 'Nice guy, quiet, never figured him for a fairy.' It was a blue-collar neighborhood, not the picture of progressiveness, but not a particularly dangerous area. Damn, it was hot that day."

Now his eyes were open, but he was not seeing the present. Lambert waited. He was somewhere else now.

"We were at one of the last houses on the block. It was a nice looking two-story—nicer than most of the other houses.

An orange cat was sitting on a windowsill on the front of the house. We had walked all the way down one side of the street and looped back up the other side, so we were near where we had parked the car. I wanted to grab a drink from my water bottle, so I told Alex to wait a second. He said he'd go see if anyone was home and for me to catch up when I could. So, I let him go up to the house alone. I never should have..."

Channing slowly shook his head, then continued, "I got to the car, took a drink, and my cell phone rang. It was Mary. She wanted to know if I had decided what kind of bushes we were going to have the landscaper put in the front yard. We talked for maybe five or six minutes, I told her I loved her, and then I headed to the two-story. Alex had already gone inside."

Lambert watched him intently. He was not upset. He was just reciting the story, but she had the impression that he had not told it before. There was a distant look in his eyes.

"The front door was cracked open. I knocked, but no one answered. I pushed the door open and yelled for Alex. When he didn't answer, I stepped inside and called his name again. I put my hand on my gun, but thought maybe Alex had gone to a back room with whoever lived there and he just didn't hear me. I checked the entire first floor. I was about to head upstairs, when I thought I heard something behind a door off the side of the kitchen. Now I drew my gun and opened the door. The steps led down to a dimly lit basement and I heard shuffling noises. I crouched and slow-walked down the wooden steps—you know the type, unfinished basement steps. I was about halfway down when I saw a black dress shoe—the kind Alex had been wearing—laying on the concrete floor. I was walking down the stairs sideways when I felt something grab my ankle and I went headfirst the rest of the way down the stairs.

"When I woke, I couldn't see much out of my left eye and my face felt wet. I looked down and saw blood on my left leg. I was sitting in a chair opposite Alex. But Alex wasn't in a chair. He was tied to a giant round circle that once was the top of a table. He was naked, in the upright position, his arms spread out like some sort of Vitruvian Man, his wrists and ankles held in place by rusty chains. Alex was conscious, but barely.

I looked around the room the best I could. I had no idea how long I had been out, but it must have been a while. The basement was damp and smelled of mold and urine. Tools lay around everywhere, in piles on workbenches, spread out on the floor. I tried to move, but my hands were tied behind my back and my ankles were chained to the chair. I called to Alex and his head moved, but he didn't answer. At some point I passed out again."

Channing got up and rolled his head around, stretching his neck. He walked unsteadily over to a wall where another picture hung. It was a picture of him with his former partner, Alex Belmont.

"A bucket of cold water got thrown in my face and I heard Alex talking to someone. He was saying that we were cops and that more cops were coming. A voice to my left said that our car had already been moved and that he doubted anyone would be bothering us. Alex, who had been the best man at my wedding and had worked midnight shift patrol with me, cursed and threatened the man, but got only silence in return. My eyes cleared up enough to make out the figure that was standing off to the side. He was well over six feet tall, must have weighed two-forty. I thought he looked Indian or Pakistani. Later I learned that he was of Sri Lankan decent, but was born in this country, so he had no detectible accent.

Channing turned toward Lambert and focused his red and tired eyes on hers. "You know, in the movies, the psychopaths always talk a lot. They use scary phrases and have a flair for the theatrical. Not this guy. He just picked up an eight-inch knife, walked over to Alex, and went to work. The piercing squeals echoed off the walls. First, he cut off his nipples. Then he skinned—"

Seeing Lambert cringe and tense up, Channing stopped himself.

Slightly embarrassed for being so graphic, Channing hesitated, and then continued. "Anyway. This went on for a while. I have no idea how long. The entire time, I was tied to that chair. I yelled and eventually pleaded for him—Jayakody, Kasun Jayakody was his name—to stop, but he didn't even acknowledge me. Eventually, Alex passed out and stopped screaming. That's when Jayakody spoke to me for the first time. He told me, 'You'll be next, but let me give you a little taste of what's to come.' Then he ripped my shirt open and went to work on me with a different knife. This one was curved and razor sharp. It cut through my skin like it was tissue paper. It was probably a few minutes, but it seemed like an eternity. I just kept thinking about my wife and how I wasn't going to see her again.

"When I woke up again, I was still in the chair, and Alex was awake and chained to that table. Everything was the same, except Alex was facing the table, his back exposed. Blood was everywhere: on us, the floor, the walls. The air was heavy with blood and sweat. I asked Alex where the man had gone. He was able to turn his head to the right enough for me to see his right ear was missing. Alex said he didn't know. He was crying. I struggled against my restraints, and every part of my chest and shoulders hurt. I tried to reassure him that we would be found, that we had marked out in the neighborhood, that cops would flood the area and go door to door. But I knew that if our captor played it cool and presented himself right to any cop knocking on the door, it could be days before we would be found—if at all."

Lambert stared at the keys in her hands. She could not look at her partner now. She had opened a door she was not ready for, and she knew it.

"Alex and I talked for a while. I told him it was all my fault. I should have gone to that door with him. He was so young."

Channing wiped his eyes and reflexively felt for the flask inside his jacket, but slowly withdrew an empty hand from his breast.

"Did you know he was the youngest person in the department to ever make it to Homicide?"

Lambert shook her head, but did not make eye contact with him.

"Yeah…people forgot that about him." Channing paused and took in a deep breath. Then, he continued, "Anyway, it wasn't long before Jayakody was back. This time he used an assortment of knives on Alex's back. Some looked new, but most were old and rusty. I screamed almost as loud as Alex. Eventually my voice started to fail. It must have gone on for about an hour before Alex passed out again. And just like before, Jayakody said very little. He just walked over to me, took the remaining shreds of my shirt off and started carving up my back. Before I blacked out, he told me that I'd be going up on the table when he was finished with my partner. I remember looking up at Alex…"

Tears filled Channing's eyes. He held a hand up to his

mouth and struggled to keep the vomit from coming up.

"I could see part of his spine—*his spine*. But he was still breathing. Somehow…someway, the tough S.O.B was still with me. That was the last thing I remembered for that day. From what I've been told, that was just day one out of three."

Channing moved to the couch on the side of the room and sat down. He took a moment to compose himself. He looked around the room and seemed to lose his train of thought. Then he raised his exhausted, bloodshot eyes and said quietly, "You should go now. Everyone. Everyone… should just go."

With that, Channing fell back on the couch and closed his eyes. Lambert stood motionless for half a minute, trying to find the words. She conceded there was nothing she could say—no comfort she could offer—no question that would be appropriate. She walked out the front door, closing it softly behind her. Sitting behind the wheel of her car, she realized she had two different partners. The Jackson Channing with a razor sharp intellect and passion for his job was one partner. The empty shell of a human to whom she had just spoken was another. In less than twelve hours, one of them would show up to work. She wondered which one.

STEP 6

We were entirely ready to have God remove all these defects of character.

The sound of plastic vibrating against wood caused Channing to stir. He reached above his head, found a pillow, and covered his face. The noise continued for several seconds and he ignored the vociferous buzzing. Channing was about to give in and pick his cell phone up from the coffee table when the offending racket abruptly stopped. He had just started to fall back asleep when the phone vibrated again and fell off the table and onto the floor.

Without removing the pillow from his face, he stretched his right arm down to the floor and felt around for the device. A few seconds later, he had the phone in his hand and located a button on the side that told the phone to ignore the call. He would check to see who it was later. It was too early and he was too hungover to deal with anyone. He had not known if he could even get himself drunk enough to give himself a hangover anymore. Now he knew.

He did not know how much time had passed when the

noise started again. He reached down, grabbed the phone, and pushed the button that would let him get some more rest. This time it did not work. It took another full minute before he realized the doorbell was ringing and someone was knocking at his door. Removing the pillow from his head, a beam of sunlight coming through the living room window blinded him. He squinted and pushed himself into a sitting position. Immediately, he regretted it and his forty-year-old stomach reverted to the way it felt the morning after his twenty-first birthday.

The ringing and knocking persisted while he slowly got to his feet and steadied himself. Trying his best not to vomit, he walked to the front door, peeked out the sidelights, and rubbed his eyes.

Pulling the door open a few inches, he cleared his throat and managed a low-sounding "Good morning."

"It's not morning. And it's not good."

His partner's attire was all business and so was her expression. She stared at him. He tried to return the look through a squint, but the sunlight was in his eyes.

"What are you doing here? Did something happen?"

"Yeah, you could say that. I've been calling you." She crossed her arms and tilted her head to the side. *Where did women learn that stance? Was there some class they took? Pissed Off At A Man 101? Was it an elective course?* To Channing it seemed like a lot of women majored in that field.

Not in the mood to play games, Channing refused to speak and kept looking at Lambert—or at least he tried to look at her. The pain behind his eyes was excruciating.

Finally giving in, Lambert asked him, "What time is it right now?"

Channing impatiently told her he had no idea.

"I figured as much. I'll be in the car. I brought coffee."

She stormed off his porch and walked toward the street where he assumed her car was, but he could not see that far yet.

After closing the door, he walked to the kitchen and looked at the clock on the microwave oven. It read 2:30 p.m. His shift had started at two o'clock. He breathed out a curse and headed to the bathroom to clean up.

Fifteen minutes later, he was sitting in Lambert's car, subjected to hostile silence—another skill that women learned at an early age. He had to find that course catalog somewhere.

Lambert drove north through town past Three Rivers University. Channing remembered that the university was the focal point of a series of mysterious deaths a few years earlier. Channing grabbed the paper cup of coffee from the car's cup holder and took a sip. He winced and nearly spit it back in the cup. Police station coffee. Seriously, why was it *always* so bad? He placed the cup back in the hole and stared out the window.

Without looking at his partner, Channing said, "You came by the house last night, didn't you?"

"Yes."

Channing tried to remember their conversation, but could only recall portions.

"I talked about Alex?"

"Yes."

"And the basement?"

"Some of it."

He paused before saying, "I'm not a bad man."

Lambert remained focused on the road. "I know," she replied without any hostility.

When they arrived at a rundown two-story house near Ohio River Boulevard, Channing did his best to reset his mind and concentrate on the task at hand. Then it occurred to him that he had no idea what that task was.

"Why are we here?"

Lambert checked an address in her notebook and, without looking up, replied, "Following a lead."

"What lead?"

Mockingly, Lambert said, "Oh…you want to participate? I don't want to inconvenience you or anything."

Rolling his eyes, Channing said, "Drop the attitude and tell me why we are here."

Lambert started to say something, but then stopped herself. She had dealt with bad cops before and had a mental folder of insults ready to heap upon anyone who could make her look bad because they were too lazy, apathetic, or incompetent to do a proper job. But Channing was not one of them. She remembered the zeal he showed when re-enacting the murder. And he was bright. There was no mistaking that. Behind those bloodshot eyes, there was a keen mind and a type of insightfulness that was rare. It was not just intelligence either. He was politically aware in a way she was not. He had tried to tell her that they would not be allowed to issue a lookout for a white van, but she did not listen. Her new partner gave the impression that he understood how all the parts moved together to create a working timepiece and, in spite of his lack of contributions to the current case, there was a combination of scientific analysis and intuition present in his work.

Obviously, he was a drunk, but who could blame him? She was not part of the *white-man's network*, so she did not hear all the gossip, but now she had heard enough to know the man had made a grim trip to Hell and back. She could not be surprised if he happened to bring home a few psychological souvenirs.

"We're talking to a man named Stuart Middlebury. Harris sent Terio and Belton to the brokerage firm where Culligan worked before he ran for office. They asked around to see if Culligan received any threats during his time there. His former secretary pulled out a box of letters and some emails she had printed off that contained complaints about Culligan. Apparently, toward the end of his time there, Culligan steered a bunch of investors toward the failed Cityflash scheme, hoping that if he could pump enough money into it, it would stay afloat. It didn't, and a lot of people got screwed over when the company crashed. When it came out that Culligan knew the whole scandal was about to come out and he kept advising his people to invest in Cityflash, a lot of people were irate."

"Why wasn't he ever indicted for insider trading?" asked Channing.

"I called both the District Attorney's office and the U.S. Attorney's office. The prosecutors could never prove that Culligan received any special information. Everyone knew he had a cousin with the city of Detroit who probably tipped him off, but the cousin wouldn't testify against him. Besides, when you can go after a bunch of high-profile city officials and grab big headlines, who cares about the little fish?"

Channing could not disagree.

"So this guy, Middleton—"

"Middlebury," Lambert interrupted. "He wrote the most threatening letter. There was nothing overt in the letter, but Middlebury said that Culligan should 'fear the reaper'."

"Like the song?"

His much younger partner tilted down her sunglasses and looked at him, "What?"

"You know, The Blue Oyster Cult."

She stared blankly.

"How about the Saturday Night Live skit with Christopher Walken?" He made animated gestures with both hands and yelled in his best Walken-like voice, "More cowbell! More cowbell!"

She blinked, and after a few beats said, "Do you need me to call you a doctor?"

Channing lowered his hands, grabbed the cup of police station coffee, and took a punitive swallow.

He put the cup down, then suggested, "Let's go talk to this guy."

Lambert raised both eyebrows, replaced her sunglasses, and said, "Good idea," then turned and opened the door. She got out of the car quickly, not wanting him to see the smile that was coming across her face.

— — —

It had been a long time since Mayton slept past noon. He had arrived back at his house after six o'clock and repeated the chore of cleaning the van and scrubbing his body. Not that he cared about getting caught. In fact, he expected he would eventually be captured. As long as he had time to finish his work, that was all he cared about. There was nothing for him past that point other than the afterlife, but he could not let himself think of that now.

He had given in to weakness when he stopped and prayed. He had given in to stupidity when he made that phone call. Those mistakes had almost ruined everything. A delivery truck had pulled in behind his van just as he returned from unloading Abdella's body. The driver of the truck had not seen Mayton's face, but could have read the license plate. But why would he? In a few hours, the driver might report that he had seen a van there in the early morning hours, but there was no reason for anyone to notice it. His van looked like any other delivery vehicle supplying the city with some useless item. Mayton smiled at that. In a sense, he supposed that was true.

Mayton looked at his watch. It was already three-thirty in the afternoon. He had time for a quick workout, and then he would head downtown to watch the festivities. He wished God would make him stronger—mentally. It was mistakes like this morning's that could derail him. To be the perfect servant, his imperfections would have to be removed. He had been forged in the fire, and now he had to become cold, hard, and flawless.

— — —

"Does this guy have a record?" Channing asked as the two detectives approached the house with once-white siding, now gray with patches of green mildew in various spots.

The badly-chipped sidewalk leading up to the front porch had abundant cracks from which blades of wintered-out grass peeked through. Lambert surveyed the windows on the front of the house, scanning for threats, but only finding damaged screens and partially dislodged shutters.

She led the way onto a covered entryway that housed an old refrigerator and a porch swing that at one time hung from rings.

Trying to look inside through a clouded window next to

the door, she said, "Four assault charges and some citations for disturbing the peace. I pulled the reports. Looks like mostly bar fights. Usually the same bar."

Channing stood to one side of the door and noticed an oil covered shirt balled up at his feet. The shirt bore some sort of logo and he used his foot to straighten the material enough for him to see the design. Lambert stood on the opposite side of the door, looked down at a doorbell fixture that was missing a button, and proceeded to knock.

The design on the shirt was somehow familiar to Channing.

He continued to unfold it with his foot and a sense of urgency crept into his voice as he asked, "What bar?"

Lambert was knocking again, this time more loudly.

She yelled, "Mr. Middlebury? Stuart Middlebury?"

"What bar?" Channing repeated.

"What? Oh...some place called Truwicks down in Sewickley."

Channing heard a floorboard creak behind the door. He quickly strode across the doorway, grabbed his partner by the arm, and violently pulled her down the steps of the porch.

"What are you doing?" she asked as she yanked her arm away from him.

Channing remained silent, his eyes on the door, and drew his newly issued GLOCK. Reflexively, Lambert mirrored his actions and took a position of concealment behind one of the rotting posts holding up the porch roof.

Channing knelt on the ground and aimed his GLOCK at the door.

In a voice that was not quite his, Channing announced, "Middlebury! It's the Sherriff's Department! We ain't here to arrest ya!"

Lambert shifted her eyes from the door to Channing. What was he up to? And why in God's name was he talking like that? Using that accent, he sounded like some sort of redneck. And the *Sherriff's* Department?

"My partner's goin' back to the car! Then, I want you to open the door and talk ta me, but I don't wanna see no gun in your hands, okay?"

A voice came through the door.

"Alright. But you ain't gonna haul me off?"

"No sir. Just wanna talk to you. Heard you got robbed by a snake named Culligan. We're try'n to figure out how many people he scammed."

The detectives heard a muffled thud as Middlebury set something down on the floor.

Without looking at Lambert, Channing commanded, "Walk back to the car and keep your eyes on those windows."

"I'm not—"

"Do it now."

It was the way he said it that stopped her from arguing. His voice was dead calm, but there was no mistaking the life-or-death tone behind his words. She walked backwards to the car, her eyes moving from one dirt-streaked window to the next, and had repeated the pattern several times by the time she took a position of cover behind the vehicle's engine block.

With a low squeak, the door opened a few inches.

"Come on out," Channing said. "When I see your hands are empty, I'll put the gun away."

The door swung open and a scraggly man wearing ripped jeans and a twenty-year-old Harley Davidson T-shirt emerged. Middlebury stood no taller than five foot four and was less than one-hundred-fifty pounds. Channing tried to imagine the diminutive man dragging a body around and tossing it off a bridge. Of course, he could have had help.

Looking at Channing, the man held up his hands to show they were empty and took two steps out onto the porch.

"He didn't rip me off. I never had no money to invest in nothin'. It was my mama. Took all her savings."

Channing lowered his weapon, but did not place it back in the holster. He backed up into the front yard, inviting the man to follow. The rush of adrenaline had temporarily relieved his headache, but now he felt the weight of his own head again.

"Where you from, officer?"

Channing started to correct him by stating his actual title, but thought better of it.

"Wheeling."

The rough man, who was fifty, but looked seventy, nodded with some level of approval.

"Moved up here to find work, ended up doin' this," explained Channing.

Middlebury gave a little smile, understanding the need to move to wherever the work was. He walked down the steps of the porch and stood in the yard, fifteen feet from Channing.

From her position, Lambert could barely hear the conversation, but she thought she heard her partner say he was from Wheeling. *Wheeling, West Virginia?* What on earth was he talking about? She did not know much about him, but she knew he was originally from somewhere around Cincinnati and had gone to college in North Carolina.

"I guess you wanna know if I killed that snake oil salesman," said the little man. "I saw it on the TV. Can't say I'm sorry."

Ideally, Channing would not have conducted the interview while standing in the man's front yard, holding a gun at his side, but he knew there was no way Middlebury would let him in the house, much less allow himself to be put in an interview room.

"So…did ya kill him? Nobody would really blame ya for it."

The rough man turned his head and spit in the direction of a broken cinder block.

"Nah. You kill a white politician and some nigger takes his place. What's the use?"

Lambert still could not hear what was going on, but she could see the man was unarmed and seemed to be cooperating. She held her weapon at her side and started walking around the car.

Channing saw something in Middlebury's expression change and his hand tightened around his pistol. Middlebury took a step back toward the doorway and Channing turned toward Lambert.

Holding up a hand, he yelled, "Stop. We're fine. Go back to the car."

She was not some rookie. In fact, this was her case. That was right. It was *her* case, and a drunk who could not even make it to work on time was yanking her around and giving orders. She continued her path into the yard.

Again, Channing told her to stop, but she was not going to play second fiddle to anyone. This was her chance to make a name for herself. She had her career path all planned out: sergeant by thirty, lieutenant by thirty-five, captain by forty— and so on until chief by forty-five. Even if she only made it somewhere close to the top in this place, she could always jump ship, head over to some other department as a chief.

She had her plan and this boozer and the rest of the boy's club were not going to hold her back. She advanced.

Realizing his partner was not going to veer off, Channing turned his attention back to Middlebury, who was walking backwards, making a slow retreat to the house. Without hesitation, Channing took off in a dead sprint toward the man, who then turned and ran in the direction of his home. Middlebury reached his doorway and was stretching his arm around the corner when Channing, running at a speed he did not think he could obtain anymore, leveled him with a shoulder. The shotgun positioned behind the door fell to the floor as both men tumbled through the living room, sliding a small rug out of place.

Both men got to their feet at the same time and Middlebury sized up his opponent. Channing stood a good eight inches taller, but having been involved in countless fights throughout his life, Middlebury decided to take his chances. Assuming a boxer's stance, the wiry man circled Channing and made several faints, attempting to get Channing to react and open himself up for a punch.

Channing holstered the pistol that had been in his hand and said, "Come on, Stuart. Now I've got to take you in. You shouldn't have gone for the gun."

Middlebury continued his dance around Channing. Lambert arrived in the doorway and aimed her gun at the man who was circling her partner.

Looking at Channing, Middlebury screamed, "Come on, cop! You can't shoot me! I ain't got no gun now. You and me gonna have to fight it out. Unless you're gonna let the nigger girl do your fighting for you."

Again, Channing attempted to convince the man to come along peacefully, and received a string of curses as a reply.

"Look, Stuart. I've got a killer headache. I'm tired. If my partner shoots you, I'll be filling out paperwork for a month, and we all know you didn't kill Culligan."

Now Middlebury was bouncing up and down as he circled. His breathing became labored. "Maybe I did. Maybe me and the boys lynched him," he said while firing a menacing look at Lambert. "Like we would do to her if things was right in this country. Maybe I stood on that bridge and listened to him beg before his neck snapped at the end of that rope. We had to make a statement. Time for the white people in this city to rise up against the Jew oppress—"

Channing bent over and grabbed the end of the rug that lay at his feet. The other end was planted firmly under Middlebury's size eights. In one swift motion, Channing yanked the rug, flipping the older man upside down. The paranoid racist's head pounded against the wooden floor and he lost consciousness. The man's chest heaved up and down, his respiratory system still trying to recover from all the bouncing around. Channing reached in his pocket and retrieved his cell phone.

"I'll call an ambulance. Would you mind cuffing him before he wakes up?"

Shaking her head in astonishment, Lambert holstered her weapon and grabbed her cuffs.

— — —

Andy Lach was on his fourth glass of wine. He rarely had more than a few sips, but today he would indulge himself. Andriy Mykhailo Lach and his parents left their Ukrainian village when he was just nine years old. His father, Pavlo, had relatives working in the steel mills of Pittsburgh and promised jobs were available for those who were not afraid of hard work. By the time the only son of Pavlo was eleven, he was going to school during the week and spending the weekends unloading produce from trucks that pulled into the city's Strip District.

By the early 1960s, Andriy, or Andy as he now preferred, was on his own and looking for work. The wholesale produce suppliers were losing out to supermarkets and the need for manual labor was declining. At least he only had to worry about himself. His father—and the steel mills—had died off a few years prior and his mother followed shortly thereafter. He had been sitting down by the Allegheny River reading the want ads when he overheard some men talking about the Incline. Apparently, that old cable car contraption on the side of Mt. Washington was opening up again.

The heavier of the men said, "Well, there you go. Maybe you can drive one of those things. It'd be hard for you to wreck one of those!"

The men laughed hard and continued talking about the thinner man's poor driving, but Andy's mind was already racing.

Well, somebody must drive those things? Why not me?

The next morning, the unemployed Ukrainian immigrant with a high school education was standing at the Duquesne Incline station waiting for someone to arrive. Within an hour, a man in a suit was unlocking the door to the station. Andy approached him and tried to hide his accent as he asked him if any work was available. Perhaps he could drive one of the cars up and down the hill?

The man in the suit laughed and told him to come inside. The station smelled of fresh paint and sawdust. The man explained that the renovations were nearly complete and led

Andy to a small room full of buttons and switches.
Immediately, Andy understood and felt like an idiot. Nobody
actually *drove* the cars up and down the hill. It was all
controlled from here. The man demonstrated how the
machines worked and the cars went into motion. The man
told him that he had one position left to fill and asked Andy
if he thought he could handle the work. Without hesitation,
Andy assured him that he was no stranger to hard work and
asked when he could start. A few days and many piles of
employment paperwork later, Andy was one of the operators
of the Duquesne Incline. That was fifty years ago.

Of course, Andy did not spend his entire career in that
control room. Over the years, he had moved around as an
operator, tour guide, museum manager, marketing associate,
and several other jobs. But it was not until five years ago that
he completely retired and stopped working at the Incline.
And now, today, here he was: the son of an immigrant steel
worker being honored in a way that was once unimaginable
to him. A new Incline car was being unveiled and on the
front of it the words would read, *The Andy Lach Incline Car.*
The guest of honor stood at the base of the hill among the
distinguished crowd of attendees. Carson Street had been
closed off and catering tents had been set up. *In a little while,
some of the city's most important people will cheer as the new car is
uncovered and begins its first official journey down the hill,* Andy
thought. He smiled and looked into his empty glass. *Maybe one
more for an old man. Tonight is my night.*

— — —

The ambulance pulled away and Channing stood talking to
a uniformed officer who stopped by to see if he could be of

any assistance. The conversation ended and Channing walked back to the car where Lambert was leaning against the passenger side door.

She brought her eyes up to meet his and asked, "How did you know?"

"How did I know what?"

"How did you know he was a crazy racist?"

"You told me."

Her expression became quizzical.

"The bar you mentioned. You said Middlebury had been arrested at Truwicks. Sometimes white supremacist types frequent that bar. Usually just a few loners who drink too much and mouth off, but sometimes the organized nut jobs and militia groups go in there. My guess is our friend Stuart is somewhere in between."

"You said the bar is *sometimes* frequented by these guys. You couldn't have known for sure he was one."

Channing nodded in agreement.

"I didn't know for sure, but there was an old T-shirt on the porch. I kicked it around until I could see the logo on it. The logo is for the Mountaineer Militia out of West Virginia. Usually they are fairly harmless, but a while back they plotted to blow up some government buildings. I figured he could be a transplanted member, or more likely, a wannabe. I doubt many true members would allow a shirt bearing their emblem to be used as an oily rag. Regardless, I had a feeling he was not going to react well to a female, African-American detective who works for a big city. For whatever reason, these guys recognize county authorities more than any other. It has something to do with their skewed interpretation of common law or some nonsense. So, I told a little…*white* lie."

This time Lambert could not help but show him a little

smile.

"So, that was why you said you were from Wheeling?"

In his best Appalachian dialect, he said, "Yeees ma'am."

Returning to his geographically neutral form of speech, he said, "Wheeling isn't so far south that I can't imitate the accent. In fact, a lot of people there really don't have an accent, unless they live out in the sticks. It seemed like a safe bet at the time."

Lambert took in a deep breath. She could still smell the booze on him. She reached in her pocket and pulled out a pack of gum.

"Here. It won't do much good, but it will help. You should probably try to stay away from other people."

His eyes fell to the pack of gum and then to the ground. He took the pack, withdrew a stick, and handed it back.

She put the gum back into her pocket and said, "Are you seeing anyone?"

His eyes shot up, his mouth opened and he fumbled for words.

"No…I mean, are you in AA? Some sort of counseling?"

Relieved, Channing said, "No." He started to say something else, but stopped.

"I know you know all the clichés. 'You can't help someone who doesn't want to be helped' and all that. It's obvious that you're a good cop. I know you've been through a lot, and I won't pretend to understand what you are going through, but my question to you is: Are you ready to get better? Are you ready to get yourself right again?"

Channing looked back at his partner and, for once, he did not see judgment in her eyes.

"Honestly, I don't know."

Lambert nodded and said, "Well, we better get to the

hospital and see how little Hitler is doing."

She started to walk around to the driver's side of the car when her phone rang. She listened intently, and then she looked across the roof of the car. Channing stared back. Her eyes were as big as pancakes and she was not breathing. Channing held his breath and waited. Whatever it was, he knew they would not be going to the hospital.

— — —

Lambert and Channing saw several patrol cars parked in a disorganized fashion all along the Carson Street station of the Duquesne Incline as they sped toward the scene. An ambulance with lights blazing and siren blaring pulled away. Lambert pulled off the road into some gravel and both detectives jumped out of the car. It took them a minute to locate the patrol sergeant who was attempting to coordinate securing the area.

"Is this one yours?" he reflexively asked Channing, who was obviously the senior of the two detectives standing in front of him."

Lambert answered, "Looks like it. Sergeant Harris just told us to head down here and that there might be a city official involved."

Not looking at her, but turning further toward Channing, he said, "Yeah, like the Culligan thing, right?"

Channing crossed his arms in front of him and said, "Are you on disability, Sergeant?"

"Uh…no. Why?"

"Because my partner, *lead* Detective Lambert must be talking into your bad ear."

The sergeant's face reddened in the cold air and he turned

to Lambert.

"Here is what we've got so far...*lead* Detective Lambert. Some of the witnesses IDed the vic as Tedla Abdella, Executive Director of the city's Housing Authority. I just got a quick look at him, but looks like he's been dead a while and he's covered with dry blood. The head of the Port Authority—which owns this thing, who knew?—said that he could have been up there all night; and the next thing you know, he's coming down the mountain in style."

Neither detective reacted to the officer's flippancy.

"Anyway, we set up a perime—"

Lambert interrupted, "Sergeant, we just got here. What are you talking about, coming down the mountain?"

The sergeant leaned back a little and assumed a posture that said, *Oh, so you guys don't really know shit, do you?*

Pointing over to the station at the base of the hill, he said "Well, *lead* Detective, the vic is right over there. Why don't you go *detect* a little and see for yourself."

Ignoring the shot, Lambert started walking toward the station at the base of the hill.

Channing started to follow, but the sergeant reached out and grabbed his arm. Recognition came over the man's face and he said, "Oh, man. You're Jackson Channing, aren't you? Geez...look, I didn't mean any disrespect. I guess with all that shit that happened to you, they probably got you taking it easy and mentoring her or something, am I right? Oh, man. I heard you were good people. I heard you got all cut up and shit. You healing okay?"

Channing reached across and removed the sergeant's hand from his arm. He said, "Actually, I'm hurting a little right now and I was wondering if you could help me with something."

"Sure thing, boss! What do you need?"

"Well, one of the areas that got all cut up was my ass. I was thinking you could kiss it for me."

With that, Channing walked away.

Behind him, he could hear the offended man yell, "Dick!"

Channing helpfully added, "tective."

Channing rubbed his aching forehead as he walked. He was starting to think that maybe the old Jackson Channing was in there after all.

Channing found Lambert standing in front of the lower station. He walked up beside her and words failed him. Both detectives looked at the shiny new Incline car. Strapped to the front of the car was the body of Tedla Abdella, an expression of pure terror permanently frozen onto his face.

A woman in a long trench coat was talking to several Port Authority employees, telling them to check the city's other Incline and to assist the police any way they could. The detectives walked over to the woman and identified themselves. When she turned toward them, the detectives could see there were tears on her face.

"I'm Lydia Vantree. I'm the CEO of the Port Authority. This is terrible—just terrible."

"Ms. Vantree, my partner and I just got here. Were you here when the body…when everybody saw the body?"

Crying harder, she answered, "Yes. I helped put all this together. My God, what a disaster. The poor man. That poor, poor man."

Between sobs, the detectives were able to ascertain that the event was to dedicate a new Incline car named after Andy Lach who had worked at the Incline for several decades. The attendees were a mixture of city officials, those who contributed financially to the preserve the Incline, and many of Mr. Lach's friends.

Channing said, "If you don't mind me asking, isn't five o'clock in the afternoon on a frigid weekday a strange time to have an outdoor party?"

The sobbing slowed and a kind smile came upon Vantree's lips.

She said, "We told Andy—Mr. Lach—that it was symbolic since he started working at the Incline on this date fifty years ago, and five o'clock was when his first shift started. But, the truth is, his health had been failing recently and I feared he might not be around in the spring."

With that, the tears came back and the CEO held a ball of tissues to her face.

Channing paused to let her collect herself, but she resumed talking. "We just painted Andy's name on the front of the car two days ago and covered the entire car so we could have a dramatic unveiling today. I talked to the operator who was on duty yesterday and he said he uncovered the car early yesterday morning, tested things out to make sure nothing went wrong during today's ceremony, and then re-covered the car late yesterday morning. He said he inspected the car from top to bottom and nothing had been touched. And then...then today the car starts down the hill, and the giant tarp that was attached to a post at the top comes off as the car descends. At first, nobody could tell what was on the front. Then, when it was about halfway down the hill, I heard a woman scream. Then more screams. Then..."

Channing turned his head and his eyes found the body. Even from this distance, he could see blood pooled heavily in two areas of the chest and what appeared to be a large gash across the man's throat. Channing noted the contortion of the corpse. Abdella's lower body was flat against the car, but his upper body was turned to the right, facing the Allegheny River—the same general direction Culligan's body had been facing. Coincidence?

Channing's mind began to race. *Was this killer playing some sort of game? Did he find the reactions of the crowds amusing? Was he watching now?* The anxiety Channing felt when standing near Culligan's corpse had been replaced with something else. Channing was starting to experience an emotion he had not felt toward anyone else but himself for a long time. He was getting mad.

Turning back to the head of the Port Authority he asked, "Ms. Vantree, I'm sorry to ask you this now, but what was your connection to Mr. Abdella?"

She gave him a blank look and asked, "Who?"

"Tedla Abdella. The victim."

With surprised eyes she responded, "That's Tedla Abdella? From the Housing Authority? My God, I didn't even recognize him. Especially the way he's all twisted up."

There was a pause and Channing became lost in thought. It was Vantree who broke the silence.

"Why did you ask me what my connection was to Mr. Abdella? I didn't even really know him. I think I met him once or twice."

Seeing her partner's mind was elsewhere and that he may not have processed the question, Lambert jumped in.

As gently as she could, Lambert asked, "Ms. Vantree, I think we assumed you knew the victim was Mr. Abdella and that you may have been friends with him because you are so upset. I know this seems like a disaster now, but nobody can blame you for this."

The woman blew her nose into some tissues and shook her head wildly.

"I don't care about how this looks. And, not to sound insensitive, but I didn't really know Mr. Abdella. I'm upset because of Andy. Poor Andy. That poor, poor man."

"What happened to Andy, Ms. Vantree?" Lambert asked.

"His heart. When people started screaming he looked up and saw the car. He was right beside me and turned to me. His mouth opened and then he just fell to his knees, then…. They took him away in an ambulance, but I know he was already gone."

The crying became uncontrollable and Lambert put a comforting hand on the grieving woman's arm and asked her if she wanted to sit down.

Lambert was leading her away from Channing when he heard her say, "He came here with nothing. All the man did was work hard his entire life. Now he dies on the biggest day of his life. The poor man. The poor, poor man."

Channing walked over to the station and looked at Abdella's body, still strapped to the car. Behind Channing was the city's skyline. It would have been starting to get dark when the car began its journey down the hill, but with the lights lining the Incline, half the city's corporate population could have seen this spectacle. Another city official. Another purposeful kill. A message sent down from the mountain?

Lambert returned from placing Lydia Vantree in a chair and was standing behind Channing. She did not say anything, but he knew she was there.

Without turning around he said, "I'm ready to get myself right and catch this guy."

Lambert looked at the back of her partner's head and said, "It could be more than one."

"No. It's one guy." Channing stared into the dead man's eyes and continued, "He's alone, he's been wronged, and he is seriously pissed off."

STEP 7

We humbly asked Him to remove our shortcomings.

A homeless man approached the section of the sidewalk in front of the bench where Mayton sat—a bench he planned on visiting again. Mayton lowered the binoculars and waited for the broken man to pass. Once the transient was gone, he resumed his watch, using the binoculars to focus on the faces in the crowd. Some of the onlookers were crying; others were in shock. Although Point State Park was all the way across the Monongahela River from the base of the Duquesne Incline, the lights from the gaggle of police cars allowed him to see the effects of his actions.

Nearly everything had gone perfectly—the build-up, the dramatic unveiling, and then the horror. They would remember this. Even though most did not understand the message yet, they would eventually. One person was getting the message for sure. Mayton read it on that person's face when the screaming started. Even at a distance, Mayton could see fear in those weak eyes. Mayton knew what the person was thinking: *It could have been me.*

Mayton lowered the binoculars again and recounted the event. Two things concerned him. A minor issue was the positioning of Abdella's body. Mayton had intentionally faced him down the river—to that place. He held onto the body and positioned it in a manner where rigor mortis would set in, making Abdella's dead eyes face a specific direction. The arms had to be stretched out so he could tie the body to the car.

The first thing that bothered Mayton was how the body appeared as it made the slow crawl down the steep grade. The body, with arms stretched out, legs hanging down and ankles crossed, looked to be in a pose of crucifixion. That was not his intention, and now he wondered if some recess in his mind had caused him to position the body in that way. This was troubling to him, but he pushed it aside.

Of greater concern was the man in the ambulance that pulled away. Mayton had not been focusing on that part of the crowd and tents obstructed some areas of the street, but he believed he had caught glimpses of a man being attended to by paramedics. He did not know who the man was, or his condition, but his work causing collateral damage was not something he had accounted for. Sure, the families of his victims would suffer, but why should they not feel the pain of losing a loved one the way he felt it every day. But nobody else was supposed to get hurt.

Once again raising the binoculars, Mayton scanned the landscape and looked at officers ducking under yellow crime scene tape. Then, between two of the tents he saw a woman talking to a slender man in a suit and a black woman. They held notepads and were taking notes. Mayton figured the two must be detectives interviewing witnesses. He started to lower the binoculars when something clicked in his memory. He adjusted the focus on the binoculars and sharpened the image of the white detective. Even from that distance, Mayton recognized the face. *What was his name? What was it? Channing. That was the name. He was all over the news a few months ago. The torture story.* In fact, Mayton was so touched by the man's plight, he sent a card to the man using the police department address, wishing him well and telling him that God works in mysterious ways. Of course, hundreds of other people would have done the same. If there was any man that would understand how far this city had fallen, it was that man. Now the hero was chasing…him?

After packing up the binoculars, Mayton stood from the bench and cut across the park, heading back downtown to retrieve his van. Watching the ground scroll in front of his feet while thinking about the ambulance and the hero cop, he felt sick to his stomach. It was not supposed to be like this. *He* was not the bad guy. He caught himself starting to pray, but stopped. *No. This is the trap. This is my weakness. Compassion and memories. Those have been my weaknesses.*

He would not—*could* not—pray to God for help. Vengeance was his new solace. Faith in vengeance would help him carry on and drown out the voices of sympathy that could hinder him. If his acts resulted in unintended victims, then so be it. His mission was bigger than one person—or ten. They had to listen. Mayton arrived back at his van, got behind the wheel, closed his eyes, and waited for the guilt to pass. He started the car and drove to his empty home, his empty life. *Somebody* had to pay for the dead, black space in his heart. He had paid enough.

– – –

Three hours after first arriving at the Carson Street Incline station, Channing and Lambert were back in the Homicide Squad room. They, along with a slew of other detectives who had been called in, managed to interview dozens of witnesses. Lambert and Channing had also tracked down the Incline operator who Lydia Vantree said had tested out the new car the day before the ceremony. Lambert had gotten the man's phone number from Vantree, then called and asked him to meet her at the Carson Street station. He was initially reluctant, saying it was his day off, and wanted to know what it was all about. When Lambert told him about the murder, he did not show much interest. When Lambert also mentioned that Andy Lach had been taken away in an ambulance after an apparent heart attack, Mason Preger told her he would be there in ten minutes.

Preger's story was identical to Vantree's. He had uncovered the car, checked every part of it—including the newly painted name of Andy Lach—run the car up and down the slope, and replaced the cover over the car.

"There sure as hell wasn't no dead guy on the front of that thing. I would have noticed that!" Preger told the detectives. "Did you guys hear anything about Andy? That man's a gem. He'd give you the shirt off his back and then some."

The detectives had already verified what Lydia Vantree had told them: Andriy Mykhailo Lach, age seventy-three, was dead on arrival at Allegheny General Hospital at 5:27 p.m., the victim of an overdue heart attack. Medication for a serious heart condition was found in his jacket pocket, along with some spare change. The detectives knew all of this, but could not release the information until it was determined if Lach had any next of kin.

"They took him to Allegheny General," was all Channing

could say.

The detectives had left the area as the crime scene techs finished looking for and collecting physical evidence. The Medical Examiner's office had already hauled away Abdella's contorted form—another life reduced to a dispassionate autopsy.

Channing sat in the chair across from Lambert. The squad room was empty. All the other detectives were either off duty, still talking to witnesses, or on other cases. Lambert's meticulously organized desk filled the space between them. Both remained silent, lost in their own thoughts and overwhelmed by the day's events.

It was Lambert who broke the silence.

"What happened to you after the first day?"

The question hung there like Abdella's corpse on the front of the car. Channing started to ask what she meant, but he knew.

"I'm sure you heard."

"I'm sure I did, but not from you."

Channing turned his head and looked at a clock on the wall. It read 9:03.

"How much did I tell you when you came by my house?"

Lambert shrugged. "Enough that I understand why you drink. Enough that I don't understand why you're back. Enough to know you feel guilty, but shouldn't."

Channing combed a hand through his hair, stood up, and paced the small space between cluttered desks.

"Are you sure you want to hear this?"

"If you think you can tell it."

Sitting on the edge of one of the desks, Channing swallowed hard and organized his thoughts. Looking at his partner, he decided to spare her the most gruesome details, but there was no way of avoiding some of the revolting facts.

"On the second day, Jayakody woke me up with a blow torch."

Channing saw Lambert's eyes dart to the desk as she tensed. He stopped to give her a chance to change her mind, but after a moment, she looked at him and nodded for him to continue.

"I was chained to the upright table top. He must have taken me out of the chair, laid the tabletop on the floor, rolled me onto it, chained me to the wood, and then propped everything up against the wall. When I opened my eyes and screamed, his eyes stared right back at me. Jayakody didn't seem to be taking pleasure in my suffering. He never seemed to take pleasure in it. For him, it all seemed…matter of fact, if you can believe that. He simply burned a spot on my abdomen to give me a jolt, and then he started in with some knives and a box cutter."

Channing decided to stop there with the description of his torture. It was a memory he did not want to have, much less inject into someone else's mind.

"Alex was crumpled up in a corner and looked to be asleep. He wasn't even tied up—no need at that point since he was obviously too weak to stand, much less run. Jayakody worked on me for an hour, maybe two, until I passed out again. I woke later and vaguely remember him unchaining me, flipping me over, and chaining me up again, to expose my back. Then, he said something about running late and told me he'd be back in a while. I heard him move toward a workbench and pick up what sounded like keys and drop them into his pocket. I assumed they were for the padlocks on the chains. Then, I heard his footsteps going up the stairs into the house. Whatever it was he was running late for, it must have kept him longer than expected, because he didn't come back that day."

I couldn't see Alex, but I heard him breathing. I talked to him as much as I could. I asked him if he could move. He came around enough that he was able to speak a little."

Channing put a hand up to his neck and unnecessarily cleared his throat.

"Our throats were so dry by then, even whispers hurt. We had only been given a few sips of water up to that point."

Channing stood up from the desk and resumed pacing.

"Alex told me he couldn't move his arms and he thought his Achilles tendons had been cut. He tried to roll over and yelped from the pain. I knew he wouldn't make it much longer. He'd lost too much blood and he said he was freezing. His body was going into shock and I doubted he would live through the night."

With no small amount of shame, Channing admitted, "Truth be told, I hoped he wouldn't. He was disfigured beyond recognition and was suffering every second."

Channing skipped over several of the hours that followed. He remembered both he and Alex crying. The apologies each of them made to the other. The praying they did together. That was just for them.

"Jayakody didn't come back until the next morning. He spent some time doing some more damage on my back, and then choked me until I lost consciousness. The next thing I knew, I was laying where Alex had been and Alex was back on the tabletop. Jayakody wasn't in the room. The tabletop was lying on the floor, nearly ten feet from me. Alex had burns on his chest and abdomen, and I could smell burnt flesh. The blowtorch was next to his feet. Alex's head was swinging side to side and he was mumbling something. I tried to move and was surprised that, like Alex had been when he was on the floor, I wasn't restrained. I tried to stand, but my legs were too weak.

It took me several minutes and I nearly passed out from the pain, but I finally was able to slide over toward Alex. He couldn't see me, but I let him know I was there. I tried to make out what he was saying, but most of it was gibberish. Then I thought I caught four words that made sense. I leaned in closer. He inhaled deeply and the words fought to get out of his mouth. Alex said, "*He...left...the...keys.*" I looked up toward the workbench where Jayakody had placed the keys previously.

From my position on the floor, it was hard to tell, but just off the edge of the bench, I could see a flash of silver. A set of keys were barely visible. Can you believe that? Through near total blindness, unimaginable pain, and paralyzing fear, Alex noticed that Jayakody hadn't pocketed the keys as he had done before. I told Alex I was going to go for the keys and I started to slide away. Without warning, Alex shot his left arm out, extending a rust-covered chain to its limits, and he grabbed my wrist. He said something else, but I told him to save his breath and I'd come back with the keys. I patted his hand and started pushing myself along the floor with my arms. The workbench was only a short distance away, but it might have been a mile. Eventually, I made it."

Channing interrupted his pacing and stood squarely in front of Lambert's desk. He waited for her reaction.

Lambert looked at him and recognition slowly registered on her face.

"He...he was alive when you made it to the keys."

Channing did not respond. The two detectives stared at each other in a silence thick with revelation and understanding.

Lambert opened her mouth to speak when a door opened in the back of the squad room and an enervated-looking Harris rushed in. Channing did not break eye contact with his partner. Lambert looked away first, acknowledging Harris with a nod. Then she picked up and shuffled some papers on her desk. Harris paused, sensing he interrupted something, and then told the pair to come into his office. Without uttering a sound, the detectives followed.

"I just got off the phone with Drayson and Wyche."

Channing watched Harris situate himself behind his desk. At the mention of the Lieutenant and Captain who coordinated the activities of the Homicide Squad, Channing frowned. In his experience, when the brass got involved, things went sideways in a hurry.

Harris, in spite of spending most of his time behind a desk these days, was still, in essence, a good street cop. He was obviously uncomfortable with whatever news he was about to deliver. Automatically, his focus went to the coffee mug sitting on his desk.

"Obviously, the Culligan and Abdella killings are connected. So, it's been decided that we'll be forming a task force. It will be a combination of Homicide detectives and our Dignitary and Witness Security guys. DWS will be assigned to various city officials and will sort through any threatening letters and calls. Homicide will follow up on any leads."

Channing knew where this was going, but temporarily bit his tongue.

"We don't know for sure they are connected. Until the forensics come back, we have to assume it could be a copycat," said Lambert, not believing it herself.

Harris took his eyes off the mug long enough to give her a look that said, *Oh come on.*

Channing spoke up. "And who exactly will be heading up the task force?"

Not looking up, Harris said, "Drayson will be running it, but the lead detective will be Hatley."

At this, Channing balled up his fists.

"Hatley! That kiss-ass couldn't find a mausoleum in a cemetery!"

"It wasn't my call," said the sergeant, still looking at the mug. "You know he's close with Wyche and Drayson."

Lambert chimed in. "So that's it? We're done? The damaged poster-boy and the fresh, black face are getting thrown off the boat?"

Channing turned toward her. So she *had* realized why they had been paired up and assigned to the case. And all this time, she had kept it inside.

"You two will still be on the case. It will just be in a lower-profile capacity."

The way Harris said the last few words made Channing think that they weren't Harris's words, but someone's above him. They may not be getting thrown off the boat yet, but they were sure being told to put on their life jackets.

"Ken...I think I have a real feel for this guy. He's isolated. He's full of rage. Don't put us on the periphery on this one. We need all the Intel going through us."

Harris's eyes remained on the mug and he did not respond.

"Ken, listen to me!"

Channing's arm struck out like a snake grabbing the mug off the desk. With a powerful motion, he threw the mug against the wall to the right of the desk. All three individuals winced slightly, expecting a shattering of ceramic. Instead, the mug thudded into the wall, creating a hole, then fell harmlessly onto the carpet a few feet below the hole.

*The damn thing really **is** possessed*, thought Channing. He rolled his eyes in exacerbation. Harris and Lambert looked at the senior detective in silence. Harris stoically stood up.

"You two will still be working the case, but just the Culligan part. Keep sifting through his background and see what you can find. Keep Hatley and me informed. He will handle any press inquiries and hand out any other assignments."

Lambert turned her back to Harris and headed out the door. "This is bullshit."

Harris looked at the only other detective present in the room and nodded. "I know it is, but you know the game. It's higher profile than it was when it was just about Culligan."

"And now the powers that be have decided that having an inexperienced, black female and her drunk of a partner may not have been the best choice to head up the investigation?"

The sergeant started to feign surprise and act as if he did not know Channing was drinking heavily, but decided not to insult the man.

"Just do what you can and stay busy. There'll be more eyes on this than Hatley's."

Channing said, "Sure," and started to leave.

"And Jackson."

"Yeah."

"Can you please hand me my mug? I rather like it."

In the squad room, Channing found Lambert waiting at his desk.

"I didn't mean to call you damaged."

"You weren't lying," said Channing.

They both stood in the quiet of the room for a few long seconds, not knowing what to say.

"Let's call it a day. Tomorrow, we'll take another look at everything and figure out which direction to go."

"I guess we'll have to brief Hatley," said Lambert. The words tasted sour coming out of her mouth.

"Yeah, I guess," said Channing.

They grabbed their coats and walked through the room.

"A mausoleum in a cemetery?" asked Lambert. "An interesting analogy."

Channing shook his head. "It wasn't an analogy. He was once supposed to meet the widow of a man killed during a convenience store robbery at the cemetery where the victim was being buried. She told him, 'Just look for the mausoleum and you'll be able to find me.' When Hatley was on the phone with her arranging the meeting, he thought she said Muslim. So, he drove around the cemetery for an hour looking for anyone who might look like a Muslim. He eventually tracked her down at home that night after she had called the squad, furious at being stood up. Hatley told the guys in the squad that it wasn't his fault and that not one single person in the cemetery was even wearing a turban."

Lambert stopped walking, grabbed Channing's arm, and said, "Please tell me you're kidding."

"As Allah is my witness."

"We're screwed," she said.

"Yep," was all he could say to that.

— — —

Mayton slept well after he arrived home from viewing the

results of his efforts at the Incline. He feared the nightmare might return, but he drifted off while replaying the beautiful, slow lowering of Adbella's body over and over in his mind. The sun was just coming up when he began his exercise routine. *Forget the spiritual and focus on the physical,* he kept telling himself. Forty-five minutes later, he was standing in front of the fireplace drinking black coffee. The large print of *The Last Judgment* hung there in its thick frame. He focused on his favorite section of the piece.

He wondered if the story of St. Bartholomew being skinned alive was true. There were other stories involving drowning and crucifixion, but for some reason Michelangelo chose to depict the martyr holding his own flesh. The ferocity portrayed in Bartholomew's face said it all.

Mayton showered, shaved, and dressed. He turned on the television—something he rarely did—and watched the news coverage of the murder at the Incline. Of course, nobody was actually killed *at* the Incline, but Mayton supposed the news station decided it sounded more dramatic that way. Then, Mayton's mood fell. The reporter at the scene said that an elderly man, a man who was being honored for a life of service, had died of an apparent heart attack upon seeing the bloody display on the front of the Incline car.

"It was just his time," Mayton said aloud. "It was just his time."

He turned off the television and walked out to the shed behind his house. He needed rope from there—a lot of rope. With the proper amount of rope and a few pulleys, he could get it just right. There was no shortage of rope. Like many of the other tools he used for his mission, he spent months making the rope himself, in plain sight of others. From a large spool, he measured off the right length. As always—he measured once. He measured twice.

STEP 8

We made a list of all persons we had harmed and became willing to make amends to them all.

The sheets around him were soaked. The shivering began around three o'clock in the morning and got progressively worse. He gave in to the withdrawal symptoms at five-thirty and drank his last two remaining beers. The beers did not do much, but the alcohol hitting his bloodstream made the shaking subside enough that he could brush his teeth and clean up a bit. While shaving at the bathroom mirror, he looked at the trench works across his body, knew his back was not any better than the front. An image of Alex flashed in his head. His hands reaching for Alex. Alex, his nose mutilated, spit and blood coming out of his mouth, saying, "Please. Please."

Stop it. Just stop it, thought Channing. He dropped the razor and wiped his face. He grabbed his cell phone and tried to call Mary. As expected, he heard four rings and then the call went straight to voice mail, but at least he got to hear her recorded voice. He hung up and dialed again. Four more rings. Then, he closed his eyes and listened to the voice again. It was as soothing as a lullaby.

Channing dressed in sweatpants and a hooded Cincinnati Reds sweatshirt and went into the kitchen. He drank black coffee and ate a slice of dry toast. When he felt confident that the first piece of toast was going to stay down, he had a second. Turning on the television, he watched the early morning news coverage of the murder at the Incline. Channing seriously doubted that Abdella was killed anywhere near the Incline, but reporters were reporters and facts were expendable.

Turning off the television, he looked at a set of wooden pegs hanging next to a bookcase on the far side of the room. On the pegs hung several medals from races in which he had competed. Of course, he had not actually won any of the races, his natural athleticism had its limits, but he had finished multiple marathons, half-marathons, and other races where anyone who completed the race received a medal. He walked over to the medals and held one in his hand. It was from a race he and Mary had run in St. Louis. They had driven ten hours the day before just to get there, had a late dinner of greasy chicken wings, and made love half the night. When they arrived at the race for the seven a.m. start time, they were exhausted, but it didn't matter. They were together on an adventure and nothing else seemed important. Inexplicably, they both ran fast times that morning and found the energy to do some sightseeing that night.

Channing felt the texture of the medal. He looked at the date. Not that long ago, but a lifetime of hurt lay between then and now. She had always deserved better than him, and he knew it. He gripped the medal, wishing it were her hand and that he would never have to let it go. Putting the medal back on its peg, he took a step back and his mind drifted toward the alcohol he no longer had in his house. He started thinking about driving around to see if any place would sell it to him this early in the morning, but he stopped himself and put on a pair of running shoes instead. Sliding the hood of his sweatshirt over his head, he went out his front door and walked out to the street. Facing the rising sun, he let a chilled breeze hit his face and took one stride down the isolated street. Then another. Then another.

— — —

Mayton used the sleeve of his jacket to pull the double doors. As usual, the lobby of the New Heights Outreach office located off Frankstown Avenue was crowded and chaotic. The air smelled of cigarettes and hopelessness. The Outreach, as it was simply referred to, was a non-profit group that capitalized on human selflessness and generosity to assist those who were not only destitute, but suffering from HIV or AIDS. Hardly a face looked up when Mayton allowed the doors to close behind him. *Godless,* was the only word that came to mind. Most of the people here were suffering because they had sinned and their suffering would not be alleviated because, in this city, good Samaritans were in short supply.

"Lester, my man!" came a voice from behind the reception desk.

He slowly walked toward the desk, scanning the room for the person he was looking for.

"Jimmy."

"It's been a while. Sure glad you're back. We are hurtin' for volunteers and you and your wife would be a sight for sore eyes!"

Mayton stopped looking around the room and looked down at Jimmy. Mayton had stopped volunteering at the Outreach when Mary had gotten sick. Obviously, Jimmy had not heard that she was gone.

"I'm looking for Danny. Is he still…"

"Danny Berres?" asked Jimmy. "Yeah, he's still alive."

The twenty-seven-year-old, hippy-looking receptionist leaned in and lowered his voice. Mayton detected a hemp odor coming from him. He had never spent much time around marijuana, so he could never tell if the odor was from the woven bracelets the young man wore, or if he actually smoked the drug. *Probably both*, he thought.

"He doesn't have long now. He's at the end of it and most days he don't make it in here. We just send some meals over to him on the days he doesn't feel like coming in."

"Has he been in today?" asked Mayton.

Jimmy shook his head. "We called and checked on him today. He said he would get down here to get his food if we couldn't deliver anything to him. We really don't have the staff right now to make very many deliveries, but since he's nearing the end, I told him we'd take something over to him in a bit."

Lester tried to appear as compassionate as possible, but it was becoming harder and harder for him.

"I tell you what, Jimmy. I'd like to say goodbye to him. Why don't you give me his dinner and his address and I'll take it over to him?"

Jimmy's face lit up.

"Lester, my man! That would be fab-u-lous! He lives in the low-income housing on Lincoln. I'll get you the apartment number."

With that, the young man went to the back to retrieve a meal and an address. Mayton turned and looked at the room's inhabitants again. He saw drug addicts, homosexuals, morally loose men and women who'd had every opportunity to follow the path. Surprising even himself, Mayton thought, *Burn them all. Burn…them…all.* Maybe he would. But for now he would have to start with just one.

– – –

"Well, look what the cat dragged in!"

Detective Chester Hatley stood up from his train-wreck of a desk, knocked over a stack of papers, and stuck out a huge paw.

Channing tried to produce a smile and took Hatley's hand first. Lambert did not make the slightest effort at amicability, but shook hands more as an involuntary response than anything else.

"Sorry we have to do this on a Saturday, but you know how it is. How 'bout we step on into the conference room and let's figure out where we are on this thing. You guys grab your notes and I'll be in there in a minute."

Ten minutes later, the two original detectives from the Culligan case were still waiting in the conference room. They had not said more than a few words to each other. Lambert was trying to assess if Channing was sober. He could feel her watching him—knew she did not want to ask because part of her did not want to know. Channing could have honestly said he was sober, but he decided not to bring it up. She had no reason to believe him either way. She would have to make her own determination.

Channing wanted to get the briefing over with quickly so

he could get something to eat. He had miscalculated his toast experiment in the morning and threw up twice during his three-mile run. In spite of that, it felt good to run again. To feel his heart race due to exertion instead of a panic attack had lifted his spirits. When he had returned to his driveway, he made a bad choice by dropping to the ground to rattle off some fast push-ups. In the past, he would have been able to crank out fifty of them in less than a minute. This time, he stopped after completing only a handful. It was not muscle fatigue that stopped him, it was his skin. When he went into the *down* position during the push-ups, it felt like the maze of scars on his chest and back was ripping apart. It was not his skin anymore. He was wearing a stranger's skin. A patchwork of affliction covered his body and had infected his mind. He stood up and walked into his empty house, feeling better, but not quite adequate.

"Sorry to keep you waiting," said Hatley as he entered the room. "There's a press conference in about an hour and Captain Wyche wants me there. I think the mayor is coming over to make a statement, too. *Wooo-wheee*, this is a big one, huh? I guess you two didn't know what you were getting into when you caught the Culligan case. Well, now it's *prime time homicide!*" He said those last words like a sportscaster promoting a football game. Lambert and Channing remained silent.

Seeing his colleagues were not amused, Hatley became more serious and said, "I've read your reports. It looks like you guys couldn't come up with much." Hatley looked up from the reports and waited for the detectives to expound, but they did not.

Looking back into the stack of papers in front of him, he continued. "A white van is the only possible clue?" This time the other detectives acknowledged him, but only with nods. Looking up at the younger detectives, Hatley said, "It seems like you two didn't find much."

Channing and Lambert stared at Hatley, but did not speak.

Reading another sheet of paper, Hatley observed, "There were no similar crimes found in the system—at least not until the thing at the Incline—and forensics couldn't give us much." Hatley was talking more to himself than to his audience. Channing realized that the much older detective had not familiarized himself with much of the information until now.

"There was one guy you talked to...where is his name..., yeah, here it is...Middle something."

"Middlebury," Lambert said. "Stuart Middlebury."

Hatley squinted at the page in front of him and said, "Right. Middlebury. Damned small font. I hate trying to read these things."

"Just try to sound out the big words," said Channing.

Hatley glared at Channing for a few seconds, then returned to the reports.

"What happened with him? It says here that he was arrested for aggravated assault when you stopped him from grabbing a weapon." He looked to Channing for an answer.

"We got called away, but Sergeant Harris sent a couple of uniform guys to the hospital to officially charge him. He's got nothing to do with Culligan's murder. He's just a racist who decided to go for a gun when we were talking to him."

"What made him go for the gun?" asked Hatley.

Lambert's eyes shifted to her right and found Channing, but Channing was already answering the question.

"No reason. Middlebury is out of his mind. He's not relevant to the case...end of story."

"Fine. So, we are still at square one. Well, maybe the Abdella killing will help us out. And we have a lot more eyes on this now."

Hatley leaned back in his chair, his tie creeping up his large stomach.

"I think you two got us off to a decent start. No reason for you to worry about all this anymore, so—"

Lambert broke in with, "Harris said we are still on the case. He told us we would still be working the Culligan angle."

Hatley smirked and crossed his arms.

"Well, we can all agree it's pretty much a dead end, so I'm not sure what more you can do. I tell you what, why don't you take another look at those videos where you saw the white van. Maybe something else will jump out at you. We're setting up a tip line, so there may be some phone tips to follow up on. And when you finish with that, maybe you can go back and re-interview those people from the bank where Culligan worked before becoming a politician."

Channing momentarily thought about explaining the difference between a brokerage firm and a bank, but decided it would be futile.

"That's it?" Lambert stood up. "Watch videos that we already watched and interview people who have already been interviewed. That's our role on this *task force*?"

"Darling…I don't think you understand how these things work. Even Jackson here, with his experience, hasn't seen as much as I have. With big cases like these, it's a *team* effort. And with any team, there has to be one leader and lots of worker bees. I'll deal with coordinating the hive and constructing a case, and you two do your part."

"*Darling?*" Lambert yelled while leaning across the

conference room table, clinched fists on the cold surface.
"Did you just call me *darling?*"

Channing stood up and gently took hold of his partner's
arm.

"Let's go."

After a moment, Lambert allowed herself to be guided to
the door, then left the room first. Channing turned back to
the older detective, whose smile showed that he was
extremely proud of eliciting such a response from the female
detective.

"Hey, Hatley?"

"Yeah."

"You do realize that the bee that runs the hive is the *queen*,
right?"

Hatley's smile disappeared and Channing went to find his
partner.

Lambert stood in an empty hallway that spurred off the
opposite side of the squad room. She was staring at a trophy
case that contained group photos of the department's
homicide squad, dating back to the 1970s. Channing walked
up beside her and looked at the photographs. She did not
turn to look at him when she spoke.

"Look at all of those faces."

Channing examined the photos one by one. A majority of
the faces were male. Almost all of the faces were white.
Channing could count on one hand the number of black
females, almost all were in photographs taken in the past ten
years.

"Not a lot of them look like me, do they?"

Channing did not answer.

"I knew what I was getting into when I joined the

department. I knew I would hear it from the public and I knew I would hear it from my coworkers. I've always known that I'd be under a microscope. But, when I'm confronted with that kind of ignorance, I have to fight back. I don't think you can understand that, and I wouldn't expect you to."

Now she turned to face her partner.

"I like you, Jackson. I think you have a good heart and good intentions. You may have saved my life at Middlebury's house and you could have thrown me under the bus back there when that sexist jerk asked why Middlebury went for his gun. And I really do think you are trying to get your life together and overcome something I can't even begin to imagine. I let you lead me away from Hatley just now out of respect for you. I didn't listen to you when you told me that Harris wouldn't allow the BOLO for the van and I didn't listen to you with Middlebury, and I was wrong both times. So, this time, something in my head told me to listen to you. But let me make this very clear. I will *not* be treated like some disobedient child and sit quietly in the corner! I will *not* spin my wheels working a dead-end case while the department Men's Club moves on without me. I won't be chastised and put in my place—not by him and not by you! So, you better tell me why you pulled me away this very minute!"

Channing turned to his partner and was taken aback when he saw tears forming in her eyes. They were tears of anger, not sorrow.

"I pulled you away because we can still solve this thing. If you would have gone any further, he would have gone to Wyche or Drayson and we'd be off the case, and I don't think you want that."

"We *are* off the case! Following up dead-end leads is not working a case."

"I agree, but something Hatley said got me thinking. He said that he would be *constructing* a case. That reminded me of something I heard the night Culligan was killed. The first officer on scene told me that Culligan had been implicated in some sort of kickback scheme with a construction contractor. Evidently, it was in the news for a short amount of time, but nothing ever came of it. The officer told me that some disgruntled employee with the construction company blew the whistle on the whole thing, but nothing else happened afterwards."

Lambert dried her eyes and said, "Nothing like that came up when we were talking to the other city council members."

"No, it didn't."

"And you aren't going to mention it to Hatley?"

"No, I'm not."

"And if it ends up being relevant to the case, we could get in big trouble for not sharing that information."

"Yes, we could."

"But, if anyone could get away with it, it would probably be the hero cop who survived an indescribable hell, and the up-and-coming black, female detective with a spotless record."

"Uh-huh."

With that, the corners of Lambert's mouth started to turn up. She asked, "The information you got from the officer at the Culligan scene…do you think it might be good?"

Channing shrugged. "Probably not. The officer was a woman."

With that, they both did their best to keep their expressions serious, both failing miserably.

– – –

"There's a familiar face!"

Lambert and Channing spun their desk chairs around to search for the voice. They had been sitting at Channing's desk, using his computer to search for any old news stories about Culligan and any improprieties with a construction contractor. So far, they had been able to verify that a former employee of a company named Harper Construction had accused his old employer of entering into a conspiracy with Councilman Nicholas Culligan. The accuser, a fifty-two-year-old man from Butler, Pennsylvania named Bryan Clifton, claimed that Culligan had given Harper officials insider information regarding competing bids. Clifton had assumed Culligan received kickbacks in return, but could not verify any payments. Clifton stated that he Harper Construction terminated him after he took his concerns to his manager.

Channing stood as the smiling man approached. Two men and one woman, all of whom Channing assumed were part of the man's staff, waited across the room. Captain Wyche, looking irritated at the deviation in the route they had all been taking, stood next to the staff.

"Mr. Mayor," said Channing, as the two men shook hands.

Slowly, Lambert stood up and Mayor Marc Wirrer flashed a smile and threw out his hand.

"Marc Wirrer."

"Tina Lambert."

"You work with this guy?" Wirrer said while nodding his head toward Channing.

"I do."

"Well, you won't do any better."

Wirrer directed his attention back to Channing.

"It's been a while. Since the medal ceremony, right?"

Channing nodded, "Right."

"I hadn't heard that you were back."

"It's only been a few days. I'm still getting back in the saddle."

"Well, it's great to see you back. I assume you're helping out with all this nastiness that's going on?"

"Yes sir, we're on the task force."

The mayor showed an expression of approval. Channing was certain it was a well-practiced expression.

"Good, good! Captain Wyche has assured me that people who commit assassinations like this are usually caught very quickly."

That was the first time Channing had heard that word used in connection with the murders.

"Assassinations?"

Wirrer cocked his head slightly.

"Why, yes. I suppose that's the proper term when political figures are killed, isn't it? I mean, just because Mr. Abdella did not hold an elected office, doesn't mean the killings aren't politically driven, right? I think we have to assume that some person or persons out there can see the progress this administration has made in combating crime and poverty, and these murders are a misguided response."

"Mr. Mayor," Channing said, "I don't think you're fully aware of the effort this killer is—"

"Mr. Mayor," Captain Wyche broke in from across the squad room. "The media is set up for the press conference. I've got the head of the task force, Detective Hatley, standing by to answer any questions you have before you address the media."

Wirrer acknowledged the captain and turned back to Channing.

"That's my cue. I'm sure that with you two on the case,

this thing will be wrapped up in no time. Stop by my office sometime, Jackson," said the mayor, not meaning it. "We'll catch up."

With that, Mayor Wirrer fell in behind Wyche, and he and his staff headed toward a door leading out of the squad room. As Wyche held the door open for the mayor, he shot Channing a look that could not have been misinterpreted as anything other than contemptuous.

Alone again in the room, the detectives sat back down at Channing's desk.

"Friends with the mayor?" said Lambert with mockingly raised eyebrows. "I had no idea you were so connected."

Channing gave a slight smile and shrugged.

"I'm not. A few months ago, he hung a medal around my neck and that's the extent of our friendship. He used the whole thing to kick off his *Steel Spirit* anti-crime initiative. I'm surprised you don't remember it."

"I remember it. But the mayor acted like you two really knew each other."

Channing shook his head.

"Just being a politician, I guess. And I suppose that's why he wants to put an assassination spin on this case. Why not play the role of the brave leader standing up to the city's criminal population? It makes for good print, I suppose."

"And you don't think it's possible that there could be some element of truth to that theory?"

"No," Channing replied.

"Because these killings are too…purposeful."

Channing thought about that word. *Purposeful.*

"Yes."

"And you're convinced that whatever message the killer is trying to send, it's personal."

"Yes," answered Channing.

"Any other reason?"

Channing thought for half a minute before answering.

"Assassinations have a political goal. But, historically, the end result is the opposite of what was intended by the assassin. Julius Caesar is knifed—a series of sadistic emperors step in. Lincoln gets killed—the South is hit with harsh measures during Reconstruction. Martin Luther King is shot—he becomes a martyr and the civil rights movement carries on."

"Your point being?"

Channing lowered his head and pondered his next words.

"Have you seen anything in this killer's behavior so far that would suggest that the consequence of each and every action hasn't been thought out?"

Lambert shook her head.

"Aside from that, even the dumbest gang-banger in the Hill District knows that if you start killing city officials, any crackdown on crime is going to increase tenfold. No...these killings are indicative of restrained and calculated rage."

"You think this guy—assuming it's a man—who's been punching holes in lungs, cutting throats, and transforming bodies into grotesque billboards, has been demonstrating *restraint?*"

Channing carefully thought it over, looked at his partner, and said, "So far."

Lambert waited for Channing to expound, but nothing more came. She broke eye contact and slid the computer's keyboard in front of her. She searched for more stories about the kickback allegations against Culligan, but as Channing was informed on the night of the murder, the story seemed to lose traction and vanish from the media outlets.

"We need to talk to Bryan Clifton," Lambert suggested. "It seems odd that he threw out these accusations and then let it all go."

"Or, the reporters followed-up on the story, discovered it wasn't true, and dropped it. Journalists don't have a fondness for writing retractions and apologies."

"True," said Lambert. "I'll go run a PennDOT check on him and pull his state tax information to get an address. He may still live up in Butler. Are you up for a road trip?"

Channing said, "Absolutely. When you pull his info from the Department of Transportation database, see what kind of car he drives. And I know the Detective Sergeant there. If we need to go up there, I'll give him a courtesy call to let him know we're interviewing someone in his jurisdiction."

"And Hatley?" asked Lambert.

Channing smirked, "You heard the captain. Hatley's *very* busy briefing the mayor. We wouldn't want the *worker bees* to disturb him."

Lambert typed on the keyboard to retrieve an address for Clifton and asked, "Do you think he knows that the leader of the hive is called the *queen*?"

Channing said, "You know…I think he might."

– – –

The drive to Butler took thirty minutes. Morning traffic was light and for most of the drive, the two detectives sat in silence not wanting to address the elephant in the room. Channing knew that Lambert was debating if she should ask any more questions about Jayakody's basement. He was feeling guilty for telling her anything at all. His burden was his alone. Sharing that with his partner—whether she asked for it or not—was unfair.

Anticipating the uncomfortable trip up north, Channing had snuck a few sips from his flask prior to hopping in the car. The shaking and sweating were becoming manageable with less and less alcohol, but were still a problem to contend with. He chewed his gum and tried to stretch his legs in the limited space in front of the passenger seat. His muscles were sore from the run, but a kind of sore that gave him pleasant recollections of a time of normalcy.

Bryan Clifton's trailer was a quarter of a mile off Route 422 in the Riverfront Estates Trailer Park. Channing wondered if the facts that the community was miles from the nearest river and the diminutive muddy lots could hardly be classified estates, were even considered before the name was chosen. Lambert slowly navigated the car over a broken asphalt road that contained the remnants of speed bumps and long-ago-faded yellow road paint.

Lot 23 sat on the edge of the park. An old Ford Bronco sat off to the side. An Igloo cooler and fishing pole that looked like it hadn't been touched since the summer sat next to the wooden steps leading to the front door. Lambert pulled half the car off the road, put it in park, and read off the plate number on the Bronco. Channing pulled out a notepad and silently read the plate number he had written down earlier when checking Clifton's state Department of Transportation records.

"It's a match," Channing confirmed and opened the car door. "Let's go hear what he has to say."

Lambert took a stride up the step to the trailer. Her knuckles hit duct tape as she knocked on a storm door that mostly consisted of dirty glass held within a thin aluminum frame. She backed down the steps to allow room for the door to open. Channing saw a dingy, ripped curtain move behind a small window at the end of the trailer, and then heard footsteps coming toward the door. When the wooden door behind the storm door opened, it did not reveal Clifton, but instead a woman who had obviously been asleep.

With one hand rubbing tired eyes on a face that was probably much younger than it looked, the woman pushed open the storm door and gave the detectives a curt, "Yeah?"

Lambert pulled one side of her coat back to reveal a badge and said, "Pittsburgh Police, ma'am. We would like to talk to Bryan Clifton."

The woman yawned, scratched a head covered by blonde hair that looked like it would have the feel of a Brillo Pad, and asked, "Pittsburgh?"

"Yes, ma'am," answered Lambert.

"Bryan don't ever go down there. Whatever it is, he ain't done it."

"We're not accusing him of anything, Miss…"

"Twickle. Loretta Twickle. I'm Bryan's girlfriend."

Lambert nodded and continued, "We think he may be able to help us with a case we are working in the city. Is he home?"

Twickle started to speak, but stopped and glanced over to Channing, eyeing him suspiciously.

"You with Pittsburgh, too?"

Channing pulled back his coat to reveal his badge. "Yes, ma'am."

The groggy woman closed the storm door a few inches and said, "You can get badges anywhere. How do I know you two are the real thing?"

Channing gave the woman a disarming smile and said, "The Butler Police know we are here. If you want, call them and ask for Detective Sergeant Hopkins. He'll verify who we are. We can wait out here while you make the call."

Twickle opened the door slightly and asked, "Backhoe Hopkins?"

Channing grinned widely, shook his head, and said, "Well, not everyone can get away with calling him Backhoe. These days he insists on 'Detective' or maybe 'Darrel' if he likes you. And I'd sure want to stay on his good side."

A hint of a smile appeared on Twickle's face and she said, "He's a good man. My younger brother got busted with some stolen tractor parts. He was already on probation and was looking at doing some time. Hopkins talked to the owner of the tractor and convinced him not to press charges and let my brother do some work around his farm to make up for everything. Hopkins didn't have to do that."

Twickle looked down at her feet and seemed to be part remembering, part debating. She looked up at the detectives and said, "Bryan's over by the fairgrounds. They're building a new community center over there and the guy who got the contract is letting Bryan help out."

Channing looked at the Bronco and glanced back at Twickle who understood the unspoken question.

"I just brought the car home a while ago. I work midnights over at the hospital. One of the guys Bryan works with came by in the van and picked him up this morning."

"The van?" Lambert asked.

"You know, one of the company vans they use on jobs."

Lambert raised an eyebrow, "What color are their vans?"

Twickle thought for a moment and said, "I don't know. I've only seen white ones, but they may have more."

Lambert looked at Channing who showed no reaction.

Lambert spoke up. "Is he back working for Harper

Construction?"

Twinkle's expression immediately changed to one of anger with a trace of fear.

"Those bastards can go to hell! They're the whole reason Bryan has to go around begging to assist on simple jobs. He should be running projects, not looking for scraps of work to do."

"Ms. Twickle, do you know why Bryan stopped working for Harper Construction?" asked Channing.

The woman closed the storm door and yelled through the glass. "Why? You want to ask *why?* Why did the company have to be greedy? Why couldn't Bryan mind his own business and not ask so many questions? Why couldn't he keep his mouth shut and just do his job when he overheard the phone calls to that politician down in…"

Twickle's eyes flared with rage and she slammed an open hand onto the glass.

"That's why you're looking for Bryan, isn't it? You think he killed that son of a bitch Culligan! Get out of here and leave us alone! How much do we…do I have to lose?"

The wooden door slammed and the detectives heard muffled crying and the sound of a glass or plate thrown against a wall. Lambert looked over to Channing who signaled they should leave.

In the car, Channing pulled out his cell phone started dialing. Lambert asked, "Who are you calling?"

"Backhoe. If Clifton gets the same idea his girlfriend just had, he may run…or fight."

"We were looking at this guy as a witness. Should we be thinking suspect?"

Channing finished dialing and started speaking into the phone. He gave a quick summary to his friend with the Butler

PD and arranged to meet him in a parking lot near the fairgrounds. He hung up the phone and gave Lambert quick directions to the meeting place.

As the car pulled out of the trailer park, Channing said, "Maybe."

"What?" asked Lambert.

"He would have access to a van. He would presumably have access to ropes and pulleys. We still have no idea what kind of weapons the killer is using. Maybe some sort of construction tools we aren't familiar with?"

"Or maybe he built something with his own hands," Lambert interjected. "Something hard to identify."

"Could be," Channing agreed.

"But," Lambert replied. "There are problems with that aren't there?"

"Yes."

"It doesn't explain Abdella. As far as we know, Abdella had nothing to do with Harper Construction."

"Right," said Channing.

"And the trailer..." Lambert thought aloud.

Channing nodded. "The trailer."

"It wasn't the worst I've ever seen, but far from meticulous. There was dirt all over that door, fishing gear and a cooler out in the open—and it's much too cold to go fishing. And even without seeing the inside of the trailer, it didn't have the feel of..."

"Purposefulness," Channing finished the sentence.

"Yes," Lambert agreed. "That place was too disorganized."

The two drove along 422, watching the scenery of open fields transform into a more urban landscape as they moved closer to the fairgrounds.

"Backhoe?" said Lambert.

Channing smiled and said, "He says he's not proud of it, but secretly I think he is. Hopkins told me that when he was a teenager, he and some of his friends would drink a few beers, search the roads for construction sites, power up some of the larger pieces of equipment, and drive them around. Back then, crews would just leave the keys in the equipment out here. Who's going to steal a bulldozer or a—"

"Backhoe," said Lambert.

"Right. Well, Hopkins was apparently notorious for doing this on Saturday nights, and this one time he got really drunk and drove a backhoe right down Main Street at four in the morning. The problem was, the one cop on duty happened to be getting coffee at the only convenience store that was open, and he stood and watched as this kid drinking a beer passed by on a giant yellow backhoe."

"So, your friend the cop got his nickname from committing grand larceny."

"Not really. If the cop had simply pulled Hopkins over and took his drunk ass home or to juvie, that would have been that. But on that night, Darrel Washington Hopkins was drunker than usual. He saw that cop pull out of the convenience store parking lot and he made a turn down a one-lane road. The cop pulled in behind the backhoe, but Hopkins just kept on driving. Thus ensued the slowest pursuit in the history of the Butler Police Department. For the next six miles, Hopkins drove that monster at the furious speed of five miles per hour, until the thing ran out of gas. At one point, the officer got out of his car and tried to run up beside the thing, since his car was too big to pass, but Hopkins pelted him with beer cans and swerved all over the place. Once the backhoe died, Hopkins peacefully went off with the officer and a legend was born."

Lambert let out a little laugh and then fell silent.

"I'm jealous."

Channing waited for her to continue.

"I would never admit this to the others, but stories like that are what you miss out on when you're a black face in the department."

Channing was confused and asked, "How so?"

"Well, how did you meet this guy, Backhoe?"

Channing responded, "I was working a case where an ecstasy dealer named Jamison was killed in West Park. The main suspect lived up here. Backhoe and I found the guy, spent six hours interviewing him, and eventually got a confession. We ended up staying in touch and getting together every once and a while. When I was in the hospital, he visited every few days. He's a good man. Why do you ask?"

"Because if it had been me...if I had caught that case and come up here to God's country and paired up with some rural cop with a nickname of Backhoe, do you really think we would have hit it off to the point that he would have shared that story with me? Do you really think your friend would become friends with me, visit me if I was in the hospital? You may not see it, but there is a certain camaraderie among white cops that's exclusionary by nature. Sometimes it's not intentional, but sometimes it is." Lambert stared at the road in front of her, then slowed the car to make a turn into the parking lot adjacent to the fairgrounds. "I'm not criticizing you. I'm just saying...it makes me jealous sometimes. It's not easy for me to admit that."

Channing spotted an unmarked SUV with tinted windows in a corner of the parking lot and said, "That's the one. Pull up behind him."

The car came to a stop and Lambert reached for her door handle. She suddenly felt a hand on her right arm. Channing was looking at her with a dead serious expression.

"Tina," he said, catching Lambert off-guard with the use of her first name. "You're right. I can't imagine what it's like for you to have to battle barrier after barrier. I know psychologically, the subconscious mind tends to make one feel a certain comfort level with those who are similar in looks and behavior. It's probably the case in many of our relationships, just as it is probably the case with me a Backhoe. I'm sure it would have been different if you had caught that case and had to work with him. Backhoe and I are basically carbon copies and we were bound to feel a certain comfort level with each other. Or, as you said, a sense of camaraderie. But I want you to know that I don't ever want you to feel excluded around me. When we get out and talk to Backhoe, I don't want you to feel like you don't belong. And believe me, if I get the sense that he's treating you any different because you are black, I'll pick his ass up and throw him out into the road. Deal?"

Lambert felt reassurance as she looked in Channing's eyes and said, "Deal."

Channing started to remove his hand from her arm, patted her like a protective older brother, and said, "I'm going to go talk to him real quick, would you mind grabbing that photo of Clifton from your notebook so we can show it to Backhoe?"

"Sure," Lambert said with a gentle smile.

Channing got out of the car and started walking toward the driver's side of the SUV. Lambert reached behind her into the backseat, found her notebook, and looked down thumbing through the pages until she found the photo she had pulled from PennDOT. She heard voices and looked up to see Channing walk over to the SUV and a man emerge from the driver's seat. The man had a gun on his right hip and badge on his left. But those were not the first things Lambert noticed about him. No. The man's most notable features were that he was the size of an NFL defensive lineman and towered over her partner, and he was most certainly black.

If I get the sense that he's treating you any different because you are black, I'll pick his ass up and throw him out into the road, Channing had said. She sat with her mouth open and turned her eyes away from Backhoe to catch Channing looking at her. He gave her a half smile and a wink.

"Bastard," was the only word she could mutter between gritted teeth before getting out of the car.

– – –

Danny Berres's hand felt tiny in that of his visitor's. The warm handshake and affable greeting temporarily allowed Berres to forget his nausea. He took the food from Mayton and invited the man into his home.

As the two situated themselves into tattered chairs around a coffee table, Berres moved some magazines on the table, placed the box of food in front of him, and said, "I'm sorry the place is a mess. I don't have too much energy for cleaning these days."

Mayton dismissed the apology with a wave of the hand. "Jimmy told me things have gotten really rough lately. I'm sorry I haven't been around more."

Now it was Berres's turn to wave a boney hand of

dismissal. "You've had your own problems. We all miss Cindy. But she's with God now. I hope I'll be joining her soon."

Not likely, you abomination, thought Mayton. *How dare this man who chose to lie down with other men—. No,* Mayton told himself. *Fight it back. Stick to your purpose.*

"I hope so, too, my friend," said Mayton.

"Have you been coming down to the center again? If you've been down there, I must have missed you."

Mayton shook his head. "No. I've been doing some soul searching of my own. I've been speaking with God and trying to discover what direction He wants me to go."

Mayton stood and walked around the room. The air smelled of illness. It smelled of death.

"Have you figured it out?" asked Berres. "Do you know what God wants you to do?"

Mayton continued his walk and looped behind Berres, who suddenly felt uncomfortable having someone standing behind him. He tried to crane his neck, but his visitor was nearly out of sight.

"I think so," said Mayton. "I think I've found my calling and it may be a bit of a surprise to you."

Berres sensed movement behind him and heard the rustling of Mayton's coat. Nervously, Berres asked, "And what is your calling, Lester?"

From behind, Mayton suddenly placed one hand on the sick man's shoulder and said, "I'm going to help put an end to your troubles."

— — —

"Bryan Clifton?" asked Channing.

"That's me. Who are you?" said the man whose face matched the photograph in Lambert's hand.

"I'm Detective Channing and this is Detective Lambert. We're with the Pittsburgh Police Department. This is Detective Hopkins, with Butler PD. We'd like to have a word with you."

Clifton carefully laid down a bundle of steel rods he was carrying across the building. All around him, men were hammering, sawing, welding, wiring, and reading building plans. Channing noticed that Clifton was by far the oldest man doing manual labor.

"What's this about?"

Hopkins spoke up and suggested, "Maybe we can head down to the station and talk where it's quieter?"

Clifton shook his head. "I'm not going anywhere. What's this about? Is Loretta okay?"

"She's fine, Mr. Clifton," said Lambert. "In fact, we just saw her at your trailer. She told us where to find you."

Clifton seemed to chew on that for a moment. He figured if his girlfriend had told the cops where to find him, whatever it was could not be too bad.

"Let's go outside where I can hear better."

The four walked out to a patch of dying grass next to a set of unused sawhorses.

Clifton shivered in the cold and used a hand to block the wind while struggling to light a cigarette. Through the other half of his mouth he said, "I didn't kill that asshole Culligan, if that's what you're thinking."

Channing bunched his coat around his chest. He quickly sized up the man in front of him and sensed that he had a certain level of intelligence about him. He decided to be direct and said, "We read the articles in the papers. If what you said was true and Culligan and Harper construction were in bed together and you got fired because of what you knew, that's a strong motive."

"I forgot, what night did the prick kick it?" asked Clifton while blowing out a stream of smoke.

Channing told him the date and time.

"I was at a meeting. Give me your card and I'll call you with some names of people who can verify that."

Lambert stepped closer and said, "Mr. Clifton, it doesn't work that way. If you're just going to make some calls and get some of your friends together to establish and alibi, that's not going to help you. If it's a lie, we'll break the alibi."

"It's not a damn lie," Clifton shot back. "I just can't give you their information unless they tell me I can. That's the way it works. I'm in AA. Have been for two years. I'm sure some of the people there will have no problem talking to you, but I'm not going to give them up until they tell me I can. Hell…one of the members of my group is a cop. Mr. Butler PD here will know her."

"Fair enough," said Channing as he handed the man his business card. "If it checks out, it checks out and you don't have anything to worry about."

Clifton nodded and tapped some ashes to the ground.

"What happened at Harper?" asked Lambert. "There were a few reports that said you were accusing Harper Construction and Culligan of conspiring together, and then nothing. No follow-up reports. No court actions. No investigations on record."

Clifton threw his cigarette on the ground, and pulled out a new one and lit it. "No investigation on record. Pfffft. What a shock."

"What do you mean, Mr. Clifton?" asked Channing. "Are

you saying someone did investigate?"

Clifton looked at Channing with eyes that contained a practiced cynicism. "I guess it depends on what you call an *investigation*. Look, all I know is what I told the reporter. I was in charge of this new project in the city, alright? Then, this one day, I'm over at the main office late one night and I overhear the head of finance for the whole damn company, Chris Menster, talking on the phone. He's telling someone that the money is on the way and that there was no way he would have entered a bid that low if he hadn't gotten the info, and all that type of crap. I listened outside the door for just another minute, but from what Menster was saying, it was clear as day that he had gotten inside information on a bid for a project. And right before he hung up he said, 'Thank you, Mr. Culligan. I'll be in touch.'"

"And you took this information to your boss?" asked Lambert.

Clifton nodded and took a drag off the cigarette. "Yeah. Real bright, huh? You see, I've met the owner of the company, Robert Harper, several times. Seemed like a real stand-up guy. So, I figure if this guy Menster is doing something shady that could get the company in hot water, Harper needs to know about it. So, I tell my boss, who takes it to Harper. The next thing I know, I'm getting a severance check and a strong suggestion to not disclose any proprietary information which includes conversations overheard in the office. Well, I got the message, but I was too pissed-off to keep my mouth shut."

"So, you went to the press?" asked Channing.

"You're damn right I did. I called up a reporter for the Post-Gazette and told him the whole story. He said his editor was hesitant to run anything, because they needed some sort of corroboration. I asked him, 'How are you supposed to corroborate a conversation I overheard unless Menster talks?' He took a run at Menster, but got nothing. I guess the reporter started looking at bidding histories and saw enough suspicious stuff to run the story. But obviously, that was a waste of time."

Channing and Lambert waited, knowing the man had more to say.

Clifton looked at a spot on his hand and uttered, "They burned up her trailer."

"Whose trailer?" asked Channing.

"Loretta's. They must have figured if they went right after me when those stories started appearing, it would look suspicious. So, they did the next best thing. They torched her trailer."

Channing looked at Hopkins, who nodded and said, "I remember that." Then, looking at Clifton, asked, "Loretta Twickle?"

Clifton gave a quick, sad nod.

Hopkins turned to Lambert and Channing and explained, "It was looked at as an arson. She had a trailer a few miles from here. The detectives found traces of an accelerant, nothing rare. She works midnights, so thankfully nobody was home." Looking back to Clifton, he said, "If I recall, she was asked if she had any idea who would do it, and she wasn't very cooperative with the detectives."

Clifton now appeared more sad than angry and said, "Can you blame her? She knew I'd been getting strange phone calls ever since the stories came out. Not to mention, suddenly nobody wanted to hire me. I'd been blackballed all over the area and it doesn't take a genius to figure out they were behind it all."

Channing thought for a few seconds and said, "You said there was some kind of investigation into your accusations? We don't have any record in the department."

Lowering the last stub of his cigarette, Clifton said, "Oh, of course not. It wasn't important enough for the real cops to investigate. No, no, no. Instead, the city sends some bureaucrat with a badge up here to talk to me, but the whole time I know it's a whitewash."

Lambert asked, "Who was the person who interviewed you."

Clifton shrugged. "Lady, I have no idea. All I know is it was some joker who said he was doing a municipal investigation for the city, whatever that means. He said he'd write up the report and send it to his boss, who would send it up the chain. I guess the chain must have been attached to Jimmy Hoffa's leg, because I've sure never seen what's on the end of it."

— — —

Chad Wayland was sitting in an old recliner, watching reruns on the television. It was a common occurrence for the manager of the city's Office of Municipal Investigations, or OMI, to spend his evenings like this, watching television in the middle of his living room, comfortably resting in his favorite chair. The life-long bachelor had long ago accepted that he was not a social person and did nothing to become somebody different. He was who he was, and there was no need to put out any effort to change. Always being somewhat of a recluse could have hurt his employment prospects, but fortunately for him, as a youngster, he had entered the bureaucratic labyrinth of a mid-sized city government and quickly came to realize that common courtesy was rarely rewarded and social awkwardness was rarely noticed.

Starting as an entry-level records clerk with the city's Pension Office, Wayland had been passed around from one post to the next, never excelling in any particular area. Wayland, however, did have certain traits that made him a desirable employee in select city offices. The thin, unpretentious-looking man had been born with a complete lack of passion. At no point during his twenty-year career in the government had he done anything other than compile data and report facts in a passable manner. He had no ambitions, no strong opinions, and cared little for the end result of his work. In sum, he was an ambivalent paper-pusher who nobody found threatening.

Wayland was the perfect candidate to manage OMI, due to his reputation as a dispassionate collector of facts who could be influenced by stronger personalities. OMI's responsibilities included investigating accusations of misconduct against employees of the city, and assembling detailed, unbiased reports. However, the power of the OMI stopped there. Once an investigation concluded, the OMI simply turned the report over to the director of whatever agency had been involved in the alleged misconduct, and the director would determine if any further action was warranted. At least, that was the process on paper.

Once Wayland assumed control of OMI, the heads of the various city offices made it clear to him that it was a much more efficient process if those expected to manage an office were to have some idea what the official report might indicate. Of course, they would not hesitate to assist Wayland in *clarifying* some information by *putting it into the proper context*. Doing things that way was better for everyone involved. The managers could handle things in-house, the city could avoid bad publicity, and OMI would not be flooded with agency reports refuting the office's findings. It was a win-win for everyone involved and created a lot less hassle. Of course, Wayland immediately saw the logic in this way of thinking and agreed to unofficially allow the high-level city managers to influence OMI reports.

Wayland picked the remote control up off the arm of the recliner and mindlessly flipped through the channels. In the darkened room, the flickering light from the screen bounced off the walls. He paused when he happened upon a game show, but became frustrated when the contestants answered the questions faster than he could read them. He continued changing the channels until he hit the end of the options and reached a blank screen with blue text at the top reading, *Channel Not Purchased, Call Customer Service to Add.* Below the text, he could see his own blurry reflection. He started to press a button to bring up the channel guide when he thought he saw something move in the reflection of the screen. Instinctively, he sat up straight and peered over the back of the chair. Nothing was there. The entrance to the kitchen was dark, his front door remained closed and the few items on the narrow table beside the door were undisturbed.

What time is it? he thought while relaxing back into the chair. Glancing at the clock beside the television, he saw it had gotten very late. His eyes were tired and, if he did not get some sleep, he was going to give himself a migraine. He started to get up, but stopped. Sure it was late, but he had nowhere to be in the morning. *Aw, live a little, Chad. Another thirty minutes won't kill you.*

He settled into the plush chair again, leaned back, looked to the ceiling, and stretched his arms out to his sides. With the television silent, he thought he might fall asleep right there in the chair.

A booming voice erupted from the man looking down at him from behind the chair.

"I have the keys of Death and Hades!"

In an instant, the intruder's arms slammed something solid down on to Wayland's chest. The pain was excruciating. The oxygen fled his lungs and he hopelessly grabbed the devices that had pierced his chest. Then, even while viewing the man's upper body upside down, Wayland could see the intruder held a knife. Wayland tried to dislodge one of the objects from his chest, but could not. The man lowered the knife in front of Wayland's face and turned it back and forth. He put the blade against the terrified city official's neck, but harmlessly withdrew the knife.

The intruder leaned down and whispered the name of a location into Wayland's ear. Unbeknownst to Waylon, they were the same two words the man had said to the others. Wayland could still feel the man's warm breath on his skin as he realized the significance of those two words. When the intruder was satisfied that Wayland understood, he pressed the knife against the man's scalp and pulled back hard. Mayton shocked himself by letting loose a guttural scream he did not know he was capable of producing. The intruder repeated the act four more times and Wayland convulsed with each new wave of pain that slammed into him. Then, the intruder placed the blood-covered blade horizontally beneath Wayland's chin and slit his throat with one smooth stroke.

STEP 9

We made direct amends to such people wherever possible, except when to do so would injure them or others.

"The lab work and final forensics analysis finally came back on Culligan." Lambert appeared next to Channing's desk. She was thumbing through a set of stapled papers, squinting at the lines of text. It was six o'clock in the morning and her eyes were revolting against her. The two detectives had returned from interviewing Clifton the evening before and agreed to meet early in the morning to figure out how far down the Harper Construction path to go. Lambert glanced from the papers to rest her eyes and looked out a window to see the sun starting to come up.

"It took long enough. It's only a murder investigation," Channing grumbled and examined the photos on his desk. Spread out across the top of the desk calendar, which was still showing the wrong month, were photos of the Culligan and Abdella crime scenes. He had arranged the sets of pictures in two neat rows—both nearly panoramic views of each crime scene. He studied the positioning of the bodies, the landscape, the method of the kill.

"The time of death still looks to be consistent with Culligan being killed in the parking garage. No surprise there," Lambert said without looking up. "The two holes in his chest were definitely puncture wounds, made with something round and pointed, but not too sharp."

"Uh-huh," Channing half-acknowledged. *The kills were similar,* he thought. *But not only because they were public murders of public servants.* The bodies were both posed facing east. He had already noted that similarity, but there was something else. He could not put his finger on it.

"The dark marks we found around his wounds appear to consist of sulfur, carbon, iron, and ash." Lambert furrowed her brow. Mostly to herself, she asked, "What does that mean? Why can't the guys down there just write this stuff out in plain English? And the rope that was used to support his body was made of *hemp.* Who buys rope made of hemp?"

Channing stopped scanning the images on the desk and looked up at Lambert.

"Did you say sulfur?"

"Yes—around the wounds. Does that mean something to you? Don't tell me you've run into a weapon that leaves traces of sulfur and carbon before."

Channing's gaze returned to the photos. He focused on one that was a straight-on view of Abdella's corpse centered on the front of the Incline car.

Lambert, seeing her partner's expression, took a seat across from him. She saw sparks of revelation in his face. The same look he had when he grabbed her and demonstrated how he thought the killer was using multiple weapons was returning to his face. She watched the expression overtake him, then asked, "What is it, Jackson? What are you seeing?"

Without taking his attention off the photos, he asked, "Are you a churchgoer?"

"Not much these days, but I spent a lot of time in church when I was younger."

"Did you read the Bible much?"

Lambert's shoulders lifted and lowered. "Sure. My mother insisted on it."

Channing put the photo down, picked up a pen, and started twirling it in one hand.

"Sulfur—it's mentioned in the Bible somewhere, isn't it?"

"Yeah, I guess," his partner responded. "But usually not in a good way. The verses that talk about it are mostly referring to foul lakes or streams of sulfur, or burning rains of sulfur, along with fire and brimstone…that sort of thing."

"Does it appear as a response? Some sort of retribution or punishment for a wrong?"

Lambert took a second to recall what she had read long ago. "I think so. Punishment for the wicked, plagues on mankind, things like that."

Channing nodded and started turning some of the photos toward his partner.

"Look at the bodies," he said. "Look at the poses."

She looked at Abdella's photo and immediately saw the similarity to that of a crucifixion. Then, she looked at photos of Culligan's body hanging from the bridge. The photos were taken with the help of a telescopic lens; the photographer was on a boat in position to see the front of Culligan's body. She failed to see any Biblical reference in the image.

Channing, seeing her confusion, explained, "If I recall from the very few sermons I ever witnessed, it wasn't uncommon for the bodies of offenders to be put on display for all to see. Some offenders were hung from trees—others, nailed to crosses. It was intended to send a message to the public. 'This person crossed a line and paid the price. This could have been you.'"

Lambert gave her partner, who seemed completely sober this morning, a skeptical look.

Channing acknowledged the look and said, "I know. It's a bit of a stretch. But look what we have so far. Two men violently murdered using what I think are homemade weapons. The killer seems to be sending a message, although we don't know what that message is. Both bodies posed to face to the east. Again, we don't know what that means, but I think it's important. And Abdella's body coming down from the mountain has religious overtones as well. I think this guy is not only angry at the world, but he's applying a type of Biblical vengeance to his work."

Lambert thought about Channing's words, but her skepticism remained. "You may be jumping to conclusions. Last night, we were at least entertaining the possibility that Culligan was killed because of a construction-kickback scheme. Now, you're proposing this guy killed people because of religion."

"Not because of religion," Channing quickly responded. "No…I think he's using religious overtones because it's part of his message. Or, maybe it provides him with some level of internal rationalization. Whatever the reason, I think we have to consider it may be part of his M.O."

Lambert shook her head and said, "I still think you are making some giant leaps here. And you said you think this guy is making his own weapons. What makes you say that?"

Channing ran off the list, "Sulfur, carbon, iron, ash on weapons that are not too sharp. Correct me if I'm wrong, but doesn't the burning of coal release sulfur and carbon? And couldn't iron be shaped over a fire?"

Lambert's cell phone rang in her pocket. As she retrieved the phone, she told Channing, "I'm not saying you're wrong, but you have to admit it sounds a bit farfetched. For all we know, this guy picked up some pieces of iron at a construction site and the positions of the bodies were simply because he wanted everyone to see what he had done." With that, Lambert glanced at the phone, saw Sergeant Ken Harris's name, and hit a button to answer the call. Covering the mouthpiece, she said one more thing to her partner. "Please don't start telling people you think these killings involve religion. We're already pretty unpopular around here."

Uncovering the mouthpiece, she turned her attention to the call and announced, "Detective Lambert."

— — —

"I think these killings may involve religion," Lambert said as she and her partner stared up from their vantage point on the corner of Smallman Street and Twenty-First. A ladder truck from the fire department was slowly navigating the narrow streets two blocks from the Allegheny River.

"I think you may be right," was all Channing could say in response. Both detectives were looking nearly straight up at a bell tower of one of Pittsburgh's oldest churches. The Polish Cathedral style church was the tallest and most prominent structure in the Strip District. Behind it, the rising sun in the wintery sky cast a shadow over the front steps, where a mortified morning crowd had begun to assemble.

The ladder truck stood haphazardly parked next to the

building. Several of its tires sat on the sidewalk that stretched along the north side of the church, and firefighters began working to extend the ladder. Nobody moved with any sense of urgency, as police officers on the scene had already entered the church, climbed creaking stairs, and pushed open a set of shutters to take a closer look at what was tied to the tower. With all four limbs stretched out, the body of what appeared to be a male with blood completely covering his face was displayed on the side of the southernmost of the church's dual towers. Multiple ropes extended from the body's wrists and ankles. Gravity pulled the figure's darkened face down toward the street.

Harris, tired and doing his best to battle the cold with a cup of steaming coffee held in gloved hands, spotted his two detectives through a light flurry of snow and walked to them.

"One of the priests called it in. As soon as there was some daylight, he walked out to clean up some trash from the sidewalk and looked up when it started snowing. That's when he saw it."

Lambert waited to see if Channing was going to mention his theory about the other murders, but Channing did not seem to be in a rush to speak.

"I made all the notifications, including one to Hatley, as soon as the call came in, and I figured you two needed to see this, too."

"We're not really on the case. It's a task force problem," said Channing, still staring up at the tower.

"It's a police problem," said Harris. "And you two are still the police." Harris glanced up at the tower as the ladder from the truck swung into place.

Channing watched the ladder make its final approach. He knew the ladder truck was a precaution. If officers went out on the tower's ledge and cut the body down, there was a possibility of the corpse falling to the sidewalk one hundred and fifty feet below. Behind crime scene tape, photographers and camera crews were already clicking and recording furiously as reporters jabbered frantically into microphones.

"I know Hatley and the task force will officially be taking this one," said the sergeant. "But I believe in the NASA method when it comes to major investigations. You build in as many redundancies as possible. That way, if one mechanism fails, another one is there to carry the load. You two," he said while extending an index finger from his coffee cup, "are the fail safe if that buffoon drops the ball."

Lambert and Channing did not need clarification as to whom Harris was referring.

"Assuming we can get a quick ID on this victim, and it turns out to be another city employee, everybody who thinks they are anybody is going to be screaming for protection. How are we supposed to do that? We can't park a patrol car in front of the houses of thousands of city employees."

Channing lowered his eyes to his supervisor and said, "Hatley set up a tip line for the public to call, right?"

Harris confirmed he had.

Channing asked, "Who is collecting the call data?"

Harris thought for a moment and answered, "Sullivan and Janey have been manning the phones, and Gustavo and Belton have been following up on anything that sounds legitimate. They go into a database and mark off the false leads as they go."

Lambert asked, "How many calls have come in so far?"

"A couple hundred," Harris guessed. "But, after today, that number will double."

"Only two detectives for all those calls?" asked Lambert.

Harris looked slightly annoyed at the question, as he was ultimately responsible for allocating manpower and resources on the case. "Yeah, that's all we have available, unless you two want to start running around talking to every paranoid schizophrenic in the metro area."

Channing interrupted, "We just want to see the spreadsheet. Sullivan and Janey...their desks are over in Narcotics, right?"

Harris said, "Yeah. They're on loan to us until this is over. Why? What are you looking for in those calls?"

"I'm looking to find religion, Ken. I'm looking to find religion."

Mayton stood in the crowd of would-be churchgoers concealing his hands in his pockets. The scratching fibers of the ropes had managed to find their way around his gloves and put a series of marks on his wrists. There was sure to be some of his DNA on the ropes, but since there would be no reason as of yet for the police to collect a sample from—or even speak with—him, he was unconcerned. However, knowing that he had left physical evidence at the crime scene forced him to reconsider his plans. He anticipated that he would eventually have to move out of his—his and Cindy's— home. Now, he would accelerate his timetable.

He had not expected to be here. After he dropped Culligan off that bridge, he went straight home to clean up. He surveyed the scene at the Incline because he wanted to see if his message was getting through. But this time, he was not sure why he stayed. He told himself it was for the same reason he watched the chaos around the discovery of Abdella's lifeless form, but he knew that was not true. Now it was something else. Something sadistic. He wanted—

needed—to see the city's pain. He wanted to bathe in the fear of the people. He wanted closure from the kill.

"You can't get away with something like this."

He jolted at the voice coming from beside him. A small woman who looked to be in her seventies was looking up at Mayton.

"A person can't do something like this and not be punished. Killing someone and desecrating a church...whoever did this will pay for it in this life or the next."

Desecrating? Mayton thought. Mayton squinted at the woman. She had no idea what she was talking about. He was not desecrating anything. He was preaching. He was...prophesizing. He was punishing and enlightening, both at the same time. This woman did not understand—at least not yet.

Large, wet flakes started to fall as the flurry turned into a heavy snow. Heads tilted down and people pulled collars up. Some people in the front of the onlookers started to head to their cars, assuming there would be no service in the church until the afternoon. The woman ignored the weather and persisted with the one-sided conversation.

"It's blasphemy. That's what it is. It's pure blasphemy." She shielded her eyes from the snow, and glanced at the firefighters and police pulling the body onto the extended ladder.

The civil servants were trying to cover the body with a sheet to hide Mayton's work. "You can't hide this," he said to himself.

"No, you can't hide this from the eyes of God," said the woman while taking a scarf out of an oversized purse, and wrapping it around her thin neck.

Mayton's eyes widened. He had not meant to say that aloud. He was exhausted and not thinking straight. He could not remember the last time he had eaten. That had been happening to him lately—forgetting to eat. If he were to finish this mission, he would have to be more attentive to his health.

"I'll pray for the person responsible, but I don't know if God can forgive this. This is soulless. Simply soulless."

"What do you know?" Mayton snapped loudly. "Get away from me!"

The heads of the remaining dozen or so people in the crowd turned his way. Mayton swallowed hard, feeling the weight of the unwanted attention. His eyes darted from face to face as he took a step back from the group. Then, beyond the crowd, he saw a flash of something familiar. The sun was peaking around a corner of the church and the whiteness of the snow hurt his eyes, but he knew what he had seen. It was the face of that detective—Channing. He was only twenty yards away and the detective was staring straight ahead. The man looked directly at Mayton, mouthed something to someone Mayton could not see, and took one long stride in his direction.

— — —

Harris popped the lid off his coffee and poured the now cold contents onto the ground.

"Looking for religion, huh?" Harris shook the cup, flinging the last drops into the air. "Whatever. Just do what you two do and find this guy. My guess is our new friend up on the tower is going to have a couple of holes in his chest and a big cut across the throat. Whatever this thing is, it's not going to stop on its own."

Channing stopped listening and turned toward the crowd of bystanders across the street. Lambert was turned the same direction, trying to zero in on whoever had yelled. Their gazes followed those of the crowd members, all of which seemed to have their heads turned away from the detectives as they watched someone in the back of the group. Lambert, being several inches shorter than Channing, bobbed her head back and forth, trying to see through all the people. Channing, however, caught sight of the man who seemed to be drawing so much attention. The tall detective blinked away melting snowflakes and locked eyes with the man. In an instant, all of Channing's instincts told him something that only an experienced cop truly understands. *The guy is all wrong.*

The man seemed to be examining Channing as he slowly edged away from the others. Quietly, Channing said, "Tina, you got him?"

Lambert finally found a clear line of sight between the shoulders of two people and said, "I got him. What do you think?"

Both detectives stepped into the street, heading toward the crowd. Before Channing could respond to his partner, the man he was watching bolted down Smallman Street. Channing and Lambert followed, running through a strip of crime scene tape intended to keep the public at a distance, and then plowing through the stunned crowd. Harris, taken aback by the sudden actions of his detectives, reflexively took off after the other two, who already had a significant head start.

As Lambert and Channing emerged from the crowd, the younger of the cops said, "What are we chasing him for?"

Her partner replied, "General shadiness!"

Even while accelerating down the street of broken asphalt, Lambert shot Channing a sharp sideways glance. This street in the old commercial section of the city widened into a portion of the district lined with brick industrial-era warehouses and concrete loading docks.

In response to training and habit more than actual hope, Channing loudly identified himself as a police officer and commanded the man to stop. The man continued tearing down the street, occasionally looking to the side for some alley of escape. Seeing how the long warehouse structures continuously covered several blocks, the man darted to the left and climbed onto a waist-high platform. Within seconds, the detectives saw the man—who was wearing black work pants, a bulky gray coat, and brown work gloves—disappear into blackness through a gap between gigantic sliding doors.

With the widening of the street and the thinning out of pedestrians, Lambert's speed advantage over Channing became evident. By the time the fleeing man slid into the warehouse, the former track star was well ahead of the ill-trained distance runner. Harris, the last to begin the pursuit, was just emerging from the crowd.

Under heavy breaths, Channing tried to get his partner's attention. Feebly, he said, "Wait!" as he tried to close the distance. Lambert, however, either did not hear him or ignored the call. Channing could only watch as she effortlessly bounded onto the loading dock, drew her sidearm, and vanished into the cavernous building. In a near panic at seeing his partner—another partner—go into a building without him, Channing summoned every ounce of energy he could to sprint to the entrance. Upon arriving at the dock, Channing leapt up and placed his hands and one foot in position to propel his body onto the platform. His foot hit a patch of ice on the edge of the concrete and he slipped off, smashing his knee in the process. Wide-eyed and becoming frantic, Channing screamed his partner's first name and made a second attempt to catch up to her. Feeling blood trickling down his left leg, he managed to get himself onto the loading dock and through the open doors.

Channing's eyes struggled to adjust to the darkness of the warehouse. Only a sliver of light peered through a large painted-over window with a broken panel. Periodically, a puff of windblown snow would make it through the hole. Channing unsnapped his holster, the sound of metal pulling away from metal seeming to be unreasonably loud. Now, with his GLOCK in front of him, he listened carefully. It was faint, but he heard what sounded like the scuffing of a shoe in the distance to his right. There was just enough light that he could see he was standing in an immense room that had three exits into what he assumed were other sizable rooms. The giant warehouse was divided into several work areas. Openings appeared to his left, his right, and one several yards in front of him. Flashing back to the sight of Alex's shoe sitting on that basement floor and re-living that feeling of knowing something was very wrong, Channing hesitated and felt dizzy. He steadied himself and made the decision to charge toward the noise to his right. *Not again*, he thought. *Never again*.

Bursting through the opening, he stopped to listen. The scuffing sound was gone. This section of the building was as dimly lit as the previous. A small hole in the roof did little to illuminate the room. Channing's eyes adjusted and he could make out outlines of typical warehouse equipment and furnishings. Forklifts sat haphazardly parked throughout the room. Wooden produce crates sat tossed into disorganized piles. Tall metallic equipment cabinets lined the walls. In the spring, Channing knew, the place would be alive with activity as wholesalers set up shop on Smallman Street. This morning, the building was vacant of employees. Channing suspected a skeleton crew would arrive in a few hours to accept deliveries for the local shops. One of them must have arrived early to open the doors, or someone forgot to lock up the previous night.

In the distance, Channing heard Harris's voice coming from the main entrance. The sergeant was calling the detectives' names, trying to pinpoint their respective locations. Channing held his breath and tried to focus his hearing on the room laid out in front of him. After a few beats he started to yell back to Harris, but something stopped him. He thought he heard the sound again, coming from behind a stack of crates. Cautiously, he moved toward the pile.

Channing kept the gun leveled at the crates and took slow sidesteps to change the angle of his approach. He cringed as the sound of his shoes crunching on unseen leaves of lettuce and onion skins echoed off the walls. The sound of his own footsteps seemed to be coming from everywhere in this place. Channing could briefly see his own breath as he passed through a ray of sunlight, the vapor vanishing before he re-entered the darkness. The detective moved between the pile and a forklift, completing the circle. He had begun to lower the pistol when he detected motion behind him.

Without thinking, Channing raised his gun hand to protect his head. A steel pipe crashed into his wrist, shattering bone in the process. The gun disappeared from Channing's hand and slid into the darkness. The detective lunged back, staggering over a box as the pipe slammed into his ribs and knocked him to the ground. The last thing he saw before his world went black was the face of the man he had been pursuing. Channing had just enough time to register the fact that he was about to die at the hands of possibly the most normal-looking man he had ever seen.

He squeezed his hands around Jayakody's throat. Channing's hair was soaked with the same sweat that stung his eyes as he lay under his nemesis. Jayakody grabbed Channing's wrists and fought for air. The man was starting to pull away and Channing screamed. Then, more hands appeared on the detective's arms—not Jayakody's hands, but hands of different sizes and shades. Channing looked to the side and saw a woman who looked to be Pakistani. She was telling him to let go. Channing looked at one of his own hands, which was constricting around a throat. It was not Jayakody's throat. The man was Caucasian and was wearing a white coat. A hospital ID dangled from a lapel. Channing released his grip as an orderly rushed into the room. More hands were present now, all of them holding him down, though he had stopped fighting. Channing saw a nurse inject something into an IV tube, then drifted into the unconscious.

A voice from across the room caused him to stir. "Mr. Channing? Can you hear me?"

Channing blinked hard and raised his head. He nodded to the doctor he had tried to strangle. The nervous man was standing several feet away and looked ready to head for the door if necessary.

"My name is Doctor Liningale. You're at Allegheny General and I'm your attending physician. Do you understand?"

Channing tried to sit up and pain shot through his body.

He yelped and lay back down.

Approaching the bed, the doctor said, "Don't try to move. You have a couple of cracked ribs and a concussion. You have a broken wrist as well. We'll put a cast on it today."

Channing tried to take a deep breath and immediately regretted it. Suddenly, a thought crossed his mind and he tried to sit up again.

"Where's Lambert?" he asked loudly.

"Please, Mr. Channing. Lean back."

"Where's my partner? Where is she?" Channing's voice boomed.

The door to the room opened and a large orderly entered. Channing realized the man must have been told to wait near the door.

"Is she hurt? Is she...where is she?" Channing pleaded as he tried to get out of the bed. The orderly was immediately beside the detective, lowering him back down. Channing tried to push the man back, but the pain was too great. "Just tell me if she's okay," he begged as his eyes began to tear-up.

The door swung open again and his partner walked into the room.

"I'm fine. I'm right here."

Channing put his head back on the pillow. He uttered a breathless, "Okay," and began to calm himself.

When it became obvious that the injured detective was in control of himself, the doctor asked Lambert to leave the room so he could examine his patient. Five minutes later, the doctor and orderly were gone and Lambert was in a chair beside Channing's bed. Standing beside her, Darrel "Backhoe" Hopkins looked down at his friend.

Hopkins was the first to speak. "I'm getting real tired of visiting you in hospital rooms."

Channing allowed himself a smile and thanked his friend for coming. Lambert had called Hopkins after Channing was admitted. They asked Channing about his condition and he obliged them by giving them the rundown of his injuries.

Over the next half hour, Lambert filled Channing in, explaining what had transpired at the warehouse. Upon entering the building, Lambert lost track of the man who had run from the church, so she took a guess and headed straight ahead into another room. All she managed to do was terrify the owner of a local store who had opened the warehouse in preparation for a morning delivery. After searching that part of the warehouse, she started back toward the main entrance where she found Harris. Both of them heard some sort of commotion coming from the room to the right of the main entrance and followed. By the time they found Channing out cold with a steel pipe lying beside him, the man they had pursued was gone through a side exit. That had been yesterday morning. He had been in and out of consciousness for over a day.

"We caused a lot of excitement," said Lambert. "The press saw us chasing that man and they are asking a lot of questions. The problem is," she continued, "we don't have any answers. I don't even know why we were chasing that guy."

Channing squirmed in the bed and tried to prop his head up on a pillow.

"He was just wrong," he explained. "The man saw me looking at him and…I don't know. He was just wrong. I think he's our guy."

Lambert, having learned not to doubt her partner's hunches, said nothing.

"Who was the victim?" asked Channing.

Lambert told Channing everything she knew about Chad Wayland, including his role as the manager of the city's Office of Municipal Investigations. At the mention of OMI, Channing looked at both Lambert and Hopkins who had not forgotten Bryan Clifton's story about being interviewed by a municipal investigator. Each detective agreed that it was not a coincidence. Channing was not surprised to also learn that Wayland had the same wounds as Culligan and Abdella, with one serious exception.

"The skin and hair on his head was peeled off," Lambert told her partner.

"What?"

"Nearly all of his hair, and the skin under it, were peeled off. I think any restraint you assumed the killer had is vanishing quickly, especially if that was him hanging out at the church yesterday. He's escalating and getting careless."

Channing's mind raced. *Missing skin and hair—that means something,* he thought. He felt like he was on the edge of figuring it out when Lambert spoke again.

"Harris should be here in a minute. I should tell you, he's taking a lot of heat on this. Calling us over to the scene and then assisting us in a foot pursuit we can't explain has put him in a bad place. I heard Captain Wyche chewed him up pretty good and is talking about suspending the three of us," Lambert explained.

"The guy ran for a reason," Channing said, looking at the ceiling.

"Well, Wyche isn't the only one to point out that the guy may have simply had a warrant out for him and thought we recognized him. You have to admit, it's pretty thin."

Channing could not argue with the logic. If he were in Wyche's position and a cop with his recent history started initiating foot pursuits for questionable purposes, it would be a tough pill to swallow.

Channing's head jerked back to Lambert. "Did you say Harris is on the way?"

Lambert said he was.

Channing looked at Hopkins, who returned a knowing glance.

"You sure you want to do that?" Hopkins asked.

In response, Channing held up his broken and thickly bandaged wrist.

With surprising speed, Hopkins whipped out a knife and started cutting off the bandages. Channing winced in pain.

"What are you doing?" asked a stricken Lambert. "You've got a broken wrist!"

Hopkins finished cutting the bandage and proceeded to the foot of the bed where he found Channing's medical chart. In a flash, the entire clipboard holding the chart was stuffed under Channing's mattress.

"Would one of you knuckleheads like to fill me in?" Lambert exclaimed.

Channing flinched as he used his left hand to gently place his right wrist down beside him. He was arranging the sheets on his bed, trying to not make it obvious that he was attempting to hide the worst of the bruising from view.

Hopkins turned to Lambert and said, "A broken wrist gets you put on light duty. However, a…" he paused and looked at Channing, who took a brief break from moving the sheets around.

"Bruised bone?" the patient suggested.

"Right—a bruised bone means you go back to work and finish the case."

Lambert was beside herself. "It's his right wrist! He can't

even draw his weapon. Of course, he has to get off the street for a while."

"Actually, I'm ambidextrous." Channing interjected. "I prefer to shoot right-handed, but I'm pretty good with my left. I even own a left-handed holster."

Lambert threw up her hands in disbelief. "And the concussion? Do you think Harris can ignore the concussion?"

"What concussion?" asked Channing. "Backhoe, do you know anything about a concussion?"

With feigned confusion, Hopkins said, "Concussion? Let me check that chart again...oh my...looks like Detective Channing's chart disappeared. And with all those damned HIPAA laws, the doctors can't tell us, or anyone else, about the patient's diagnosis. Such a shame. I guess Harris and the department will have to take the detective's word for it."

Lambert stared daggers at both men.

Hopkins told Channing, "Oh, and Clifton's alibi did check out. I didn't have a lot of faith that he'd follow up with you guys, so I paid him a visit and convinced him it was in his best interest to get those names to us. It all checked out."

Channing was not surprised. His mind jumped back to Wayland.

"His body was facing more to the north than the others, wasn't it?"

Lambert said it was.

Channing leaned his head back and closed his eyes. Then, his eyes shot open. A wave of adrenaline surged through his body and his pain vanished. *How could I have not seen it?* He silently scolded himself. He spoke aloud to the other detectives. "The project Clifton was working on for Harper Construction. Where in the city was it?"

Hopkins and Lambert said they did not know.

"I do," said Channing looking at his partner. "Have you ever gone running along the Allegheny River trail?"

"Sure. I still do sometimes."

"Ever run out to Washington's Landing?"

In an instant, everything clicked for Lambert.

"My God," she said.

Channing nodded.

"Care to elaborate for those of us non-city folk?" asked the large detective from Butler.

"Along the river, there's an island just off the North Shore. The west end of the island has a community of townhomes, a business park, and a marina. The other end is heavily wooded with some open recreational areas. If you drew lines of sight from where the bodies of Culligan, Abdella, and Wayland were displayed, the lines would all run into the island: Washington's Landing."

Hopkins remained silent knowing there had to be more to Channing's excitement.

Lambert continued the explanation, "And in the middle of the business park there is a set of new office building for the city government. It was a huge construction project that took months to complete. And unless I'm mistaken, the largest of those buildings is the City Housing Authority."

Channing agreed and said, "Which was run by Tedla Abdella. And how much do you want to bet that the project was handled by Harper Construction, which received inside bidding information from Nicholas Culligan?"

Hopkins, playing devil's advocate, broke in. "Just because three bodies may have been positioned so they were facing in the general direction of the island, doesn't necessarily mean the island is the key. There are lots of points beyond that island that could be important."

Channing answered his friend. "It's called Washington's Landing for a reason. George Washington supposedly visited and slept on the island during the French and Indian War. There is a historical marker on the eastern tip of the island that mentions his visit. I've run by it a hundred times."

"And?" Hopkins asked.

"And," Lambert said, "Wayland was *scalped*."

Hopkins thought about that. "So the killer is a culturally insensitive history buff?"

Channing shook his head and said, "No. And I'm not sure it's a message anymore. Like Tina said, he's losing his ability to restrain himself. The seams are starting to come apart."

The three detectives let a silence fall over the room as they each tried to find holes in the overall logic. In the end, they concluded that if Harper Construction had worked on the municipal project on the island, then it was all too much to be a coincidence. Before they could discuss the revelation any further, Sergeant Ken Harris entered the room. Channing shifted his energy to acting as if his injuries were minor. There was no way he was going to get put behind a desk. For the first time in the investigation, he felt as if he was not running an uphill race. He was over the hump and picking up steam. He had a broken wrist, a concussion, cracked ribs, a bruised-up face, a gash on his leg, and was battling alcohol withdraw symptoms. But he finally felt like he had some momentum. In all his years, he had never failed to finish a race.

– – –

The old mattress creaked as he tossed and turned. Mayton could not believe how exhausted he was, yet he could not will himself to sleep. The pursuit through the Strip District made his decision easy. After taking out that cop and making it back to his van, he had rushed home and loaded the van with some necessities. The only non-essential item he had taken was the print of *The Last Judgment*, which was now propped against the wall beside him.

He needed sleep, but could not force it to come. His thoughts were scattered, and at times, incoherent. One moment he was swinging the pipe at that detective, the next he was hearing Cindy's voice telling him to relax. *Had he killed the detective?* If so, it had certainly not been intended. He did not have anything against the man. In fact, the man had been through an ordeal so horrible that Channing should have had an understanding of the evil that existed in people—people like Chad Wayland. But here was that detective back at work serving the same government that Culligan, Abdella, and Wayland had served. The man had been pursuing *him*, instead of seeing who the real offenders were. Mayton decided that if the detective were dead, then so be it. He was part of the same system as the others.

The fire in the wood burning stove that warmed the room was dying out. Mayton got up and resupplied the stove. He sat in a wooden rocking chair, the fire from the stove acting as the only light, and tried to quell the voices: Cindy telling him to loosen-up and live a little; his minister telling him to forgive and listen to God; God telling him—. It was then that Mayton realized he had not heard God's voice in some time. He had tried to pull away from God and succeeded. Now, it was mostly Cindy's voice that would not leave him alone.

He had to sleep. His work was nearly complete, but he had to keep control of his faculties or it would all go wrong. The Spartan room he had relocated to was cold, but he started sweating. The room had been all but forgotten by others, only used as storage during the summer months. The only items left behind were an assortment of tools, buckets of paint, and an abandoned bottle of some sort of alcohol. His heart raced and he covered his ears while rocking back and forth. Things had to slow down or it would all fall to pieces.

Mayton's eyes searched the room for anything that would calm him down. The flickering light from the stove reflected off the half-empty bottle sitting on a shelf. Mayton stood and picked up the dusty container. The worn label told him the bottle contained rum. Other than a small sampling of wine, he had never allowed alcohol to pass his lips. *But now*, he thought, *I'm free*. Hearing his dead wife imploring him to live a little, he picked up the bottle and unscrewed the top. Mayton lowered his head and sniffed the liquid. The repellant odor caused him to turn away. Noticing his hands starting to shake from fatigue, he closed his eyes and forced himself to take a drink. He coughed furiously, nearly dropping the bottle. Once he regained his composure, he took another drink, then another—each sip becoming more tolerable. Cindy had wanted him to be more like other people. Mayton now knew he had failed her in that respect. Wiping his mouth with a sleeve that was still covered in the blood of a police detective, Mayton thought, *I'll make it up to you, my dear. I have one more thing I have to do.*

— — —

The sun had set and the hospital room was unevenly illuminated by florescent lights. Hopkins and Lambert sat beside Channing's bed attempting to convince him to remain in the hospital overnight. Harris had left after being briefed by Channing and Lambert. The veteran officer was unconvinced by Channing's insistence that he would be ready to return to duty in the morning and he confirmed his suspicions when his search for a medical chart was unsuccessful. Harris had watched the three conspirators, looking for one of them to crack, then gave a gesture of surrender and headed out the door.

Hopkins stood, placing a heavy hand on his friend's shoulder.

"I'm heading back north. I'll go pay a visit to Bryan Clifton and find out what project he was working on in the city. Even if it was a different project, it doesn't mean Harper didn't have a hand in the work on the city buildings."

Once Hopkins was gone, Channing turned his head to Lambert and said, "I need you to do me a favor. Is my coat in here somewhere—maybe the closet?"

Lambert frowned. "It is, but you don't need it."

"I'm not checking out. I'll wait until morning, but I need my coat."

Channing's partner locked her eyes on to his. "I know what you want from your coat and you don't need it."

"Tina, I'm working on it. I really am, but it's going to take a while. I just need a sip from the flask in my coat pocket."

Lambert sighed and reached into her own coat pocket. "You mean this flask?"

Channing waited for an explanation.

"I didn't want the EMTs to find it on you. If they found it and showed it to Harris, or anyone else for that matter, you'd be suspended for sure."

Channing thanked her and reached for the flask. To his annoyance, Lambert held it just out of his reach.

"Let me ask you something," she said. "When I went into

that warehouse, I thought I heard you screaming from the loading dock. Were you?"

Channing explained how he hurt his knee on the platform.

"That's not what I meant," said Lambert. "I heard you scream for me to stop, and you called my name."

"All right. So what?"

"I heard something in your voice that seemed out of character for you. I heard panic. Extreme panic. Then, instead of waiting for Harris—who couldn't have been far behind you—you rushed in and managed to get yourself hurt."

"You rushed in, too," replied Channing.

"Maybe I shouldn't have, but I can't get your tone of voice out of my head. I think you saw your partner going through a door without you and you freaked out a bit. Tell me I'm wrong."

Channing said nothing.

"I'm not him," said Lambert.

Looking away, Channing mumbled, "I know that."

Placing a hand on his face and turning him back toward her, Lambert said each of her next words slowly. "You are not responsible for me."

"Yes I am. I was responsible for Alex and I'm responsible for you. If something happened to you…"

Lambert removed her hand and sat back in her chair.

"You told me Alex was alive when you got the keys to the chains."

Again, Channing turned his head away.

"The official account was that Jayakody killed Alex while you were unconscious. Then, since you were unable to climb the steps out of the basement, you found a long garden rake, positioned yourself beneath the stairs, and waited for

Jayakody to return. When he finally descended the stairs, you tripped him—the way he tripped you—and you...you took care of him with the rake."

Channing closed his eyes and saw the prongs of the rake repeatedly entering his captor's neck.

"Then, you found a cell phone on his body and called for help. But that's not what happened is it?"

Channing cleared his throat and found his partner's eyes.

"No," said Channing as he replayed that day in his mind. "Like I told you before, Alex was still alive when I got to the keys."

He could smell the dank air of the basement in his nostrils. An imagined heat on the cuts across his chest and back made him involuntarily squirm in the bed.

"I reached the keys and crawled back to Alex. He was so weak—almost too weak to cry. I started to unlock one of his wrists when he told me to stop. He knew we were both too weak to get out of that basement and he thought he was near the end. Alex said he was in so much pain—too much for anyone to stand. I tried to tell him it would be all right. "We'll find a way out of here," I lied. But he was begging me...pleading with me to...end it. My disfigured, dying friend and partner was suffering as much as anyone could suffer and he was begging me to put him out of his misery. Of course, I told him I wouldn't do it. I unlocked his wrists and then another thirty or forty minutes passed. At some point, I realized we had no idea if or when our tormentor was coming back. During that time, I crawled my way up the basement stairs, only to find the thick door locked from the other side. I returned to Alex's side. Over the next hour, Alex's begging persisted and he wore me down. I didn't have the guts to do it myself, so I leaned over him—my own blood-filled tears falling on his face, mixing with his—and I handed him a long piece of glass I had found under the steps. Alex thanked me and then my friend slit his own throat."

There was a vacant look on Channing's face and a certain kind of numbness in his voice. His speechless partner sat motionless.

"You probably know most of what happened next. A few hours after I helped Alex die, Jayakody came home. The part about me killing Jayakody and using his cell phone is true. The first officer on the scene was an old-timer named Charlton. He came through the door to the basement and found me leaning against a wall, sobbing and ranting about how I had killed my partner. He took one look at what Jayakody had done to Alex…and to me…and told me that I didn't kill Alex and that there certainly wasn't any sign of suicide. He informed me that Alex was the victim of the sick bastard laying there with metal spikes in his throat, and that I needed to keep my mouth shut until I could get my head right."

Channing came back to the present and turned back to his partner. "I don't remember much over the next couple of days. By the time I regained my senses in the hospital, my supervisor was in my room telling me the same story that Charlton had told. He made it pretty clear that he didn't want my account of what had happened. We both knew what was going on, that a lie was being constructed to protect me—and the department—but neither of us stopped it from happening."

"The supervisor was Harris?" Lambert asked.

Channing nodded.

"I was in the hospital for weeks. Of course, I stayed away from reading newspapers or watching the local news. When I was released, I discovered I was being touted as a hero for having escaped the ordeal and ridding the world of a monster. And the story wouldn't go away because it was too juicy for the press to ignore. Not only did it turn out that two serial killers unknowingly lived down the street from one another, but the same cops ended up having contact with both of them. There was no way the story was going to fade away."

Lambert sat forward. "From what you described, there is no way Alex would have lived. You did what you thought was right."

"It doesn't matter. I gave up on him. I let my friend and partner go into a house by himself and then I killed him. End of story."

"So you decided to come back to work and...what? You think you can find some sort of atonement for what you did? And you're going to blindly rush in to try to save me, even if it gets you killed? This is your plan?"

Channing did not speak.

"In your house, I saw pictures of a woman. Is that your wife?"

Channing looked at his left hand and his thumb brushed against his wedding band. "Yes, at least for now. I forced her away."

"She had to have told you that Alex's death wasn't your fault. I'm sure she tried to help you."

"She did," said Channing, lowering his hand. "But I had started drinking and taking pills. I wouldn't listen to her. Now, she won't speak to me. I don't blame her one bit. I call her cell phone a few times a week, but she never answers."

"Do you know what? I'm going to give you your flask." She laid the flask on the bed beside Channing. "Drink up if you want. But ask yourself if you should be rushing around trying get yourself killed protecting me as a way of making amends to Alex, or if your time would be better spent making amends to your wife…and to yourself. Just think about it and decide which way you want this to go."

Channing reached across his chest and picked the flask up with the hand that wore his wedding ring. In front of his face, the silver flask appeared gray under the lights.

Without looking at his partner, he placed the flask back down on the bed and said, "I'm checking out of here in the morning." He turned away from Lambert and closed his eyes. "You should get out of here and get some sleep."

Lambert started to say something, but stopped herself. She stood to leave.

"Take the flask with you," said Channing, without opening his eyes. If his eyes were open, he might have seen a small smile appear on his partner's lips as she exited the room.

STEP 10

**We continued to take personal inventory and when we
were wrong promptly admitted it.**

The tiny feet tapped across the barren floor. He was lying
on his side, his face pressed deep into the old mattress.
Hearing the sound, a drowsy eye crept open. Finding the
source of the offending noise, Mayton focused on the
creature. The mouse stopped and raised its nose into the air,
and then continued its trek along the wall. Mayton rolled over
on his back and heard the mouse skitter away, startled by his
movement.

The dryness of his mouth made him feel sicker than he
already was. He sat up, dug around in a bag he had brought
with him, and pulled out a bottle of water. After downing half
of the bottle, he lay back down, closed his eyes, and felt the
room spin. He wondered how people drank alcohol on a
regular basis.

Turning back onto his side and pulling the blankets
around him, he watched the area where the fire had gone cold
during the night. He tried to tell himself that everything was

going according to plan, but he knew something was off. Something had pulled a thread of his own consciousness, and his intellect and awareness were unraveling. How could he have been so stupid and selfish? To stand in front of that church, gawking at what he had done.

The company where he had worked considered him the expert in Quality Control. He knew better than anyone that every process has a predictable rate of failure. To reduce that rate, one has to reduce the variations in the process. It is that simple. He could not understand how he had allowed himself to get off track. *What is happening to me?* he thought. One look from that detective, and he had panicked. He may have killed that man, Channing, but regardless, now people had seen his face. Even if they did not know exactly who Mayton was, the walls were closing in on him.

Keeping his eyes closed, he finally allowed himself to wonder how things would end for him. He had intensely focused on killing those who had taken so much from him. But now that only one remained, he finally had the luxury of considering his own fate. Eventually, he would be tracked down. He knew this. But did he want to live long enough to tell his story in a courtroom, or rather let his message speak for itself? *Maybe it doesn't matter,* he thought. *When the time comes, it may not be up to me.*

For some reason, this made Mayton smile. The realization that he did not know how it would all end excited him. Pushing the heavy blankets off, he stood and rubbed his face. There, his fingers found thick stubble. The hangover he was experiencing made the rubbing sound seem louder than it was. Surprising himself, Mayton laughed aloud. His next kill would close the loop and Mayton would take his time with the victim. He would remain deaf to the cries for mercy, while inflicting a level of pain that few could imagine. Then, when he was finished, he wouldn't put the body in some spectacular location for all to see. No, he would put it in a park where the city's three rivers merge, a place where the victim could still face the scene of his evil act.

Excitement built inside of him. He wanted blood and he wanted it right then and there. Trying to calm himself, he reminded himself that he had no choice but to wait. By now, Wayland would have been identified and his target would be nervous and well protected. That was all right with Mayton. There would be no more variation in the process he had planned out and the odds of failure would be miniscule. Taking a cell phone from his bag, he dialed a number. Attempting to hide his impatience, he spoke into the phone slowly and clearly. His instructions were precise and the listener understood every last detail.

— — —

Putting her cell phone away, Lambert said, "It's Washington's Landing."

Channing nodded. Quick glances, rolling eyes, and even a few snickers had welcomed his presence in the squad room. In law enforcement, he knew it was hard to earn respect, but ridicule and condemnation came easy. Word had spread about the previous day's dubious pursuit and Channing managing to get his ass kicked at the conclusion of the chase. The already wary detectives now looked at Channing as a liability at best. Channing pushed it aside.

"That was Backhoe?"

"He talked to Clifton who verified he had been working on the Washington's Landing project," answered Lambert.

"Not only that, but Clifton said it was the only project Harper Construction had going on in the city at the time."

Channing swiveled his chair and felt pain shoot through his torso. His tightly wrapped ribcage ached with every breath. His wrist was heavily taped and the detective wore his sport coat to conceal as much of the bandage as possible. It had taken him an hour of arguing with the doctors at the hospital in the morning, and another thirty minutes of awkwardly signing waivers and release forms with his left hand, before he got out of the hospital. He had taken a cab home, changed his clothes, and then called Lambert to pick him up. He was tired, beat up, and he craved alcohol, but he continued to focus on the task at hand.

"We need to check the background of that project. What's so special about it?" asked Channing, not expecting an answer.

"I did some internet research earlier this morning. Other than a few small stories in the press about the development of the island and the new municipal buildings, I couldn't find anything."

Both detectives fell silent, waiting for a revelation to come to either of them. The silence extended as they watched a ragged-looking Harris arrive and move through the squad room. Without making eye contact with anyone, he evaporated into his office and closed the door.

"Do you think we'll all get suspended?" asked Lambert.

"I don't know," said Channing. "The brass will hold off for a few days. They would look awfully silly if they suspended us and then it turns out we were chasing the right guy. Right now, they have bigger problems. Every city official is screaming for protection and the most prominent ones are effectively in lockdown. First, the department will try to manage the crisis, then it will look for scapegoats if need be."

Lambert's head dropped, and for the first time, Channing saw a lack of confidence overwhelming his partner.

"I'm sorry."

"What for?" she asked.

"You got a bad deal all the way around. You were paired up with me on an all-or-nothing case. You had to help me carry my baggage. I unloaded a lot of personal stuff on you. And now you may take some heat because I chased a man just because he looked wrong. Not to mention, we may never find that guy since he was wearing gloves and didn't leave any prints on the pipe he used to pummel me." Half joking, he continued, "If it makes you feel any better, you could probably sue the department for setting you up to fail."

"That's it," said Lambert.

Channing held up his good hand. "Wait a second...I really don't know if you can sue. I didn't really—"

His partner cut him off. "We need to search for any court records on those properties. Maybe there was a civil action that didn't make the news. There could have been a property dispute or something like that."

Channing agreed that it was worth a shot.

Pulling car keys out of her pocket, she suggested, "Let's head over to the courthouse and dig around. Maybe we can see if there is a reason for someone to be really pissed off about that project."

Channing, who had been impatiently waiting for the tip-line records to be sent over from the detectives in the Narcotics section, pulled a sleeve down over his bandaged arm and followed his partner out the door.

– – –

The granola bar was dry and tasteless. Mayton forced himself to chew as he adjusted the rear view mirror. Even with the sparse amount of light entering the parked van, he could see how pale he was. Shoving the mirror around and taking another bite of food, he squinted to see the footpath that ran through the deserted park present itself in front of him. Taking his sleeve and wiping fog from the interior of the windshield, he waited, much like he had waited countless times before.

"Right on schedule," he said to himself as he saw a figure in the distance. The person was easily a hundred yards away from Mayton's van and, as always, paid it no attention. Not immediately seeing the other thing he had expected to see, Mayton grabbed his binoculars and raised them to his face. A second later, he adjusted the focus and two blurry images behind his target became distinguishable. The two bodyguards were trailing the target during what had traditionally been a solitary morning run. Not only were the guards present, but they appeared to be attentively scanning the area while they ran. One of them even seemed to notice the van, but stayed with his charge as the trio made a turn and disappeared from view. Mayton started the van and cranked up the heater. More fog shot up the windshield and then slowly vanished from the bottom up.

The van smelled of death, and Mayton had to admit he did not smell much better. He thought about his plan and was only slightly uncomfortable. He did not like involving variables he could not control, but he had no choice. Assuming this part of the plan went well, his mission would be completed very soon. He had left no loose ends and accounted for everything.

Well, that's not quite true, he thought. There was one other variable, but it would not be a problem. In a moment of weakness, he had done something he felt was necessary at the time, but later deemed to be careless. *No matter*, he concluded as he pressed his foot on the accelerator. Everything was already set into motion and all he had to do now was lay low and wait.

— — —

"Here's something." Lambert drew some of the papers closer to her face. "It looks like some lawsuits were filed against the city and specifically the Housing Authority."

Channing leaned closer and then drew back when a sharp pinch of pain registered with him.

"According to this, five suits were filed by city employees who worked at the Housing Authority Building on Washington's Landing. Each of them claimed they came down with various illnesses after moving into the building. They all cited environmental causes. I see one here mentioning respiratory problems, another having to do with the sudden onset of recurring anaphylactic shock, another stating the plaintiff developed vertigo and ulcers…the list goes on."

Channing took one of the papers his partner had put down on the table and read. "I don't see a disposition anywhere."

Lambert dug around in her stacks and pulled out several forms. "It looks like they were all settled by the city and Harper Construction. The terms of the settlements were not disclosed and it looks like all sorts of confidentiality agreements have been signed. Five lawsuits. Five agreements. If anyone discloses any information about the case, they forfeit their settlement." Lambert shook her head. "A cover-up."

Channing suddenly felt discouraged. With non-disclosed settlements and confidentiality agreements, this would take weeks to untangle. Lawyers would have to get involved, and he *hated* lawyers. "We don't have time for this. And these people aren't going to talk to us."

"We don't have a choice," his partner responded. "At the very least, we need to run the names of the plaintiffs through NCIC and check for criminal histories."

"Exactly what individuals were named in the suits?"

Both detectives shuffled papers, but came up empty.

"I just see organizations. I see the City of Pittsburgh, the Housing Authority, Harper Construction, and the City Planning department."

"Okay," said Channing while attempting to lean back. "Let's play it out. If the killer is one of the people who got sick, we can assume they might blame Abdella since he ran the Housing Authority. There was some initial publicity about Culligan taking kickbacks for bids, so that explains his death. Wayland would have been responsible for the investigation, which Bryan Clifton claims was a joke. So, if you were looking to get even for being sick, who would you go for next?"

"Robert Harper, the owner of Harper Construction," said Lambert.

"Right. And the City Planning Department is named, too. They would have handled the zoning for that entire project. Who runs that group?"

Lambert pulled out her phone and started typing out a search.

"A woman named Treva Pinkston is the Planning

Director."

"We need to talk to Harris and see if she's been assigned a security detail. In the meantime, we need to find Robert Harper." Searching the papers on the table, he added, "I think I saw a phone number for the company headquarters in here somewhere."

Channing stopped cold. He read and reread a paragraph above where his finger had landed. "We have a problem."

Lambert leaned over to see what had caught her partner's attention. Her expression turned sour and she went back through the stack of papers listing the plaintiffs.

"There were only five lawsuits filed. Only *five*."

Channing read the paragraph for the third time. It was on the bottom of filing by one of the plaintiffs.

On the aforementioned date, the plaintiff began working at the Housing Authority building located at 12 Washington's Landing Way, Pittsburgh, Pennsylvania. The plaintiff alleges he and five other individuals developed severe medical problems in the subsequent months and brought this to the attention of the Housing Authority. Five of these six individuals are seeking actual and punitive damages.

"Who doesn't file a lawsuit when they get seriously sick or injured?" Channing asked.

"Someone who plans on taking matters into his own hands," Lambert surmised.

It took five minutes and three call transfers for Channing before finally learned the location of the owner of Harper Construction. Only by threatening an obstruction of justice charge, did he convince the fourth person to which he spoke to surrender the information. The detectives repeatedly called Robert Harper's cell phone, only getting through to his voice mail.

Lambert's car raced across town at breakneck speed as Channing continued to dial Harper's phone number. The vehicle skidded to a stop in the gravel parking lot next to the address they had been given. The detectives jumped out of the car and moved quickly toward a construction site. The project, a new office park on the south side of the city, was mostly a shell. The framework of the structures was complete before the ground froze. All that remained to be finished was the internal workings of the complex.

Construction noise drowned out the crunching of the gravel under the detectives' feet as they closed in on what appeared to be the main construction trailer. Saws, drills, and hard voices filled the air as men moved past windows that contained no glass. Channing and Lambert spotted a group of men in hardhats standing near the trailer. The man in the center of the group, conspicuous by his dark suit and trench coat, looked up as the detectives approached. Channing noted the man did not appear to be surprised or apprehensive. To Channing, the man seemed to be expecting them. Speaking at a volume loud enough to conquer the surrounding racket, the man dismissed the group of workers and signaled for the detectives to follow him into the trailer.

Dry heat from space heaters slammed into the faces of the three individuals as they filed into the temporary office. After giving his guests adequate time to get situated, the man stuck out his hand and gave an unnecessary introduction.

"I'm Robert Harper. I assume you are with the police?"

Shaking the man's hand in turn, the detectives introduced themselves. Harper took a seat behind a beaten metal desk and invited Channing and Lambert to sit across from him in the only other chairs that fit in the cramped space.

Lambert opened her mouth to speak, but like her partner,

she sensed the man across from her had anticipated their visit. Noticing that Channing was in no rush to say anything, she leaned back and waited. Harper, a fit-looking man well into his fifties, removed his hardhat and placed it on the desk. Feeling the silence enwrap him, he made infrequent eye contact with the detectives and shifted uncomfortably in his seat.

"I knew you would be coming to see me," he stated, sounding like a beaten man.

The detectives said nothing.

With a sigh of resignation, Harper continued, "After I found out Abdella was killed, I was afraid it might be about Washington's Landing. I held out hope that Culligan and Abdella both being killed was a coincidence, but then that guy from municipal investigations ended up dead. Then I knew it was about Washington's Landing."

Harper leaned forward and combed his fingers through graying hair. Like a man tired of carrying the weight of the world on his shoulders, he said, "I know I should have called the police, but I just kept hoping I was wrong."

The dejected man's shoulders sagged and tears filled his eyes. "What can I do to help?"

Lambert answered, "Tell us about the project on Washington's Landing."

Harper tried to compose himself, took a drink of water from a bottle on his desk, and began.

"We were contracted to clean out and demolish the old buildings on the island before building the new structures. Glyco Chemical was the previous owner of most of the land being developed. They went belly-up several years ago and pretty much abandoned the facilities there, leaving equipment and all sorts of stuff."

Channing sat forward and asked, "What sorts of stuff?"

With sorrowful eyes, Harper answered, "There were unlabeled barrels of chemicals in a few buildings. We discretely removed most of them."

"Most?" asked Lambert.

Harper hesitated and then drained the rest of his water bottle. He said, "In the last building we began clearing out, we found a stockpile of barrels in a basement. Several had corroded or had otherwise spilled. The fumes hit a couple of my guys pretty hard."

"And you discretely removed them, too?" said Channing.

With widening eyes, the company owner shook his head and said, "No. It was too much stuff and it had obviously seeped into the ground. I wanted to immediately call in the state and federal environmental authorities."

"But you didn't," said Channing.

"No. I didn't. I wanted to give the city guys a heads-up because I knew it was going to delay the project for months, if not years. So, I called Tedla Abdella and told him about it. The Housing Authority was going to occupy the majority of the office space we were building and I figured he'd want to be the one to pass the word up the chain of command."

Channing asked, "What did he say?"

Harper grabbed his empty water bottle and tried to shake another drop into his mouth. He said, "He asked me who else knew about it. I told him that only a couple of my guys knew, and that they weren't feeling well. He asked me to talk to them and tell them to keep it quiet so as not to start any sort of environmental panic. Then, he asked me to keep quiet about it until he could figure out what to do next. He told me he'd call me back in a few minutes after he talked to some people."

"Did he call you back?" asked Lambert.

"No. Instead I got a call from Nick Culligan. He told me that everything was under control and that my guys could wear protective gear and handle the cleanup. Of course, I knew that wasn't right and I told him so. Even if we managed to remove all the barrels, whatever those chemicals were had to have gotten into the soil. The floor of that basement was broken apart in a million places. In some sections, there was no concrete at all—just dirt. My company isn't equipped for that type of work."

"But you went along with it, didn't you?" asked Channing.

"Culligan made it clear that the city would not be using my services any longer if I didn't go along. He also implied that I might get some future contracts—multi-million dollar contracts—the city had coming up in the next few years. He told me he and Abdella had already spoken with the head of City Planning, everyone was on the same page, and I needed to play ball."

Through a clenched jaw, Lambert said, "And you knew he could back up what he was saying, because he gave you inside information on the bid for the Washington Landing project."

Harper fell silent and stared at a wall.

For a moment, the three sat and listened to the low hum of the space heaters. Channing watched the man across from him. He wanted to be angry, but he could practically feel the regret oozing out of the man's skin. Channing decided to help finish the story.

"So the Housing Authority building opened up and people got sick. How many lives did you help put at risk? Fifty? A hundred?"

"Only a few got sick—only the ones on the first floor, right above the basement. Most of the workers were on the upper floors," explained Harper.

"What were the sick ones exposed to?" Asked Lambert. "Did you even determine what those chemicals were?"

Harper shook his head. "We have no idea. Once the complaints started, the city got attorneys involved and we issued huge settlements. It cost my company millions, but at least I didn't have to shut down and lay off all my workers. I wanted to go public, but my employees have families to support. I used up all my personal savings to pay the victims, and still had to use some company funds. Personally, I'm bankrupt—but I don't care. I know what I did and I deserve much worse than this."

The room became quiet again as each of the individuals tried to process the situation. Lambert decided to ask about the particularly troubling piece of information she and Channing had discovered at the courthouse.

"There were six victims and only five settlements. Why didn't the sixth victim file suit?"

Again, Harper became distraught and choked out, "Because she died."

"And the family didn't sue? That seems odd."

Harper did not respond.

Channing said, "You're not safe. He's coming for you. You know that, right?"

Taking a handkerchief out of his pocket and wiping his eyes, Harper said, "He's not coming for me."

Channing suddenly felt a knot form in his stomach.

"Why not?" he asked.

"Because I already told him everything he wanted to know."

Channing and Lambert stopped breathing.

Harper explained, "He showed up at my house a few

months ago and told me who he was. He looked like a train wreck and was desperate for answers. Of course, I had no idea he was capable of murder. I told him how I gave in to Abdella and Culligan. I told him how I suspected the city's investigation was a joke. I told him how we were all responsible for his wife's death. I was in pretty bad shape myself. In fact—truth be told—I was pretty drunk when he showed up. I hadn't left my house in days and was hitting the bottle pretty hard. At one point, the two of us were standing in my living room and I was crying and apologizing. He was an arms-reach away from a pair of scissors sitting on a desk. I noticed him staring at the scissors and then looking back at me. Do you know what I did? I actually turned my back to him to make myself another drink. I took my time and waited...hoped he would plunge the scissors into my back. Keeping my back to him, I told him I would never forgive myself. In the quietest voice, he said, "Your suffering will be of your own making." Slowly, I turned back toward him. He wasn't there. The front door was open and he was simply gone.

I passed out soon after he left. In the weeks afterward, I tried to tell myself it had all been some drunken dream. Then Culligan was killed—then Abdella—then Wayland. Part of me hopes he comes for me, but he won't. He knows I'm already in Hell."

"Who is he?" asked Channing.

"He's a hangman with a cause," Harper whispered to himself.

Channing stood up. "Who is he?" he repeated loudly.

Harper looked up and exhaled a troubled sigh. "Mayton. His name is Lester Mayton."

STEP 11

We sought through prayer and meditation to improve our conscious contact with God *as we understood Him*, **praying only for knowledge of His will for us and the power to carry that out.**

The battering ram splintered the lock on the door as members of the SWAT team flooded the house. Harris, Channing, and Lambert waited on the street and listened for the sound of gunfire. Five minutes passed, and the leader of the tactical unit approached the detectives and informed them nobody was in the home.

"Do you think he's on the run? Maybe trying to get out of the country?" asked Harris, not really expecting a response.

Channing and Lambert stood quietly, watching the SWAT team file out and begin to congregate next to a van.

Harris said, "We'll find him. We've got his photo, you confirmed it's the same guy we chased through the Strip District. It's just a matter of time."

"We may not have time," said Channing.

"Meaning what?" asked the sergeant.

"Harper said Culligan told him the head of City Planning was involved. Harper relayed that to Mayton."

Harris said, "She's had a full protection detail since Wayland's murder. Nobody is getting to her. All the department heads are under heavy guard until this thing's over. Besides, it's possible Culligan was lying and just wanted Harper to feel more pressure."

Channing fell silent and watched the house.

"Look—the two of you followed your instincts and identified the killer. And you get the added bonus of making those jackasses that wanted to suspend you—and me—look pretty dumb right now. I'd say you're pretty much untouchable for the moment. How often does one become untouchable? Enjoy it. It doesn't happen too—"

Harris stopped speaking as a black Crown Victoria pulled up and rocked to the side as Hatley got out.

"Are you fucking kidding me?" he yelled to the three as he approached. "I'm the head of the task force and I found out by listening to the scanner in the station that a suspect has been identified and you guys are running a tactical operation over here! Is this a joke?"

"Calm down, Hatley," ordered the sergeant. "Last I checked I'm still your supervisor and I'm not obligated to report to you. Anyway, the suspect has been identified. He's on the run and a BOLO is being issued for him and his van. Don't worry, I'm sure Captain Wyche will still give you a nice pat on the back for being such a good boy. In fact, I heard you were on the brink of cracking the case. You guys were operating under a theory that organized crime was moving into the area, right? Maybe if you're lucky, this former pharmaceutical employee—Mayton—will turn out to be a secret hit man working for La Cosa Nostra."

"Screw you, Ken! I was crackin' heads in this town while you were still in elementary school. I'm going to be sure to tell the captain how the three of you withheld information from me and did everything you could to slow down the task force. Hell, by the time I'm done telling Wyche and Drayson about how you conspired with this chick and her psycho partner, you'll be begging to keep your jobs." Turning to Lambert, he said, "Of course, I'd be doing you a favor, honey. After the way this loon got his last partner killed, I'm probably saving your life."

Channing moved forward, but Harris quickly stepped in and held Channing back.

Lambert caught Channing's gaze and said, "Untouchable?"

Channing gave a quick nod. Lambert's right fist hammered Hatley's nose, breaking it immediately. The high-pitched shriek exiting his throat caused the members of the testosterone-loaded SWAT team, who were taking off their tactical gear, to pause, take notice, and then laugh hysterically.

"You don't think he's running, do you?" asked Lambert once she and Channing were back in the squad room.

The tip line info had finally been emailed over, and Channing clicked his mouse as he scrolled through the records. He said, "I don't know. I don't think so. Mayton's still out there, and we still don't know where Abdella was actually killed. I don't like loose ends."

"What are you looking for in those records?"

"Porn."

"What?" asked Lambert.

"Porn. You know…I'll know it when I see it."

Lambert moved her chair closer to her partner. Channing caught her flexing her hand.

"It was a nice punch."

She gave out a little laugh and said, "It was an overdue punch. Do you think he'll cause trouble?"

Channing smiled and said, "No, I don't think so. Captain Wyche is a pragmatist and deep down he knows Hatley's an idiot. And by now, the SWAT fellas have told half the department about Hatley squealing loud enough to break glass. No...I think we'll be fine."

Lambert put a hand on Channing's shoulder. He turned away from the screen and met her eyes. She said, "Jackson, you should get out of here."

Channing turned back to the monitor and said, "I don't much feel like going home. It's...hollow."

"I didn't say you should go home. You should go talk to your wife. I assume you still love her."

"Very much."

"Then go get her."

"I'll call her later tonight."

"No, don't call her. Go find her."

Channing said, "No, I owe her too much to do that. If she's ready to talk to me, then she'll talk to me. But I'm not going to force anything on her. I've done enough damage."

"Fine. Then call her. Call her now."

Channing began to argue, but stopped himself. He pulled out his cell phone and began to dial. Before he pushed three digits, Harris broke out of his office and exclaimed, "We got him! We've got Mayton!"

The smell hit Channing before he saw anything. Nothing smelled quite like burned flesh. Lambert covered her mouth and nose with one arm and extended her flashlight with the other. Both detectives weaved between the trees and bushes, moving toward the other flashlights. Through the beams of light, smoke drifted off the body as it smoldered. Up a hill in the distance, floodlights illuminated the deck on the back of a house. According to Harris, it was the home of the city's Planning Director, Treva Pinkston.

Channing spotted the man he knew was a member of the department's Dignitary and Witness Security squad and approached him. James Specter was wiry man in his forties who had come from a Special Forces background in the military. Channing knew him from his patrol days and liked the man.

"Is this your doing, Jim?"

At seeing Channing, Specter allowed himself a rare grin and shook his friend's hand. "As much as I'd like to claim I scared the guy to the point of spontaneous combustion, I can't claim this one."

Channing smiled back, but Specter could see it was forced. Channing asked, "Can you tell me what happened here?"

"This guy tried to get in the back door of the house. I was making my rounds around the perimeter when I spotted him. He was dressed all in black, was wearing a mask, and carrying a gym bag. I drew down on him, identified myself, and ordered him to the ground. He took off running through the woods, I used the radio to let the other guys here know what was going on, and I chased him while the rest of the detail secured the Planning Director. I pursued him to this point when he turned and dumped a container of gasoline all over himself. He must have been carrying it in the bag. Anyway, I'm yelling for him to stop and get down on the ground, but he finishes with the gas and then uses a lighter that I hadn't even seen in his hand. Then…poof! He's screaming and rolling on the ground, but what can I do? I don't have any way of putting the guy out and you can see how far it is to the house. For a second, I thought of shooting the guy just to put him out of his misery. It took a minute, but he finally stopped screaming and I went back up to the house and got a fire extinguisher. Of course, by the time I got back, he was toast and the fire was pretty much out."

Channing asked, "How did you ID him?"

"The gym bag didn't burn too much. We found a wallet with his driver's license, credit cards, and some other things. There were a few other items in the bag that were a little strange. First, I thought they were burglary tools, but one of those things sure looks like a blade."

Channing's eyes followed the direction Specter was pointing and Lambert, who had been listening to the two men, pointed her flashlight in that direction. The detectives saw two long spikes and a knife. Channing noted the knife did not appear to have a distinct handle, as the entire implement was made of some sort of metal. Each of the handcrafted items was as black as the night.

Specter continued, "We each had a picture of Mayton, but as you can see, the body is in bad shape. The mask he was wearing was some sort of synthetic material and melted to his face. However, he looks to be roughly the same height as Mayton."

Channing stared at the body, his mind sorting through the new information.

"How's Ms. Pinkston?" Lambert asked Specter.

"She's pretty rattled. Between you and me, she strikes me as a bit of an emotional wreck. I get the impression she was pretty fragile even before people started telling her she needed a protection detail. As soon as she found out what happened out here tonight, she popped a couple Ambien and went to bed."

Channing thanked Specter and walked away, his partner following.

"It's not him, is it?" asked Lambert, realizing they were walking back to her car.

"No."

"A diversion? While he escapes?"

Channing thought for moment and said, "I don't know—maybe."

Dead leaves crackled under their feet as they walked up a steep hill, the voices from the crime scene growing fainter. The smell of winter replaced the stench of death. As they ascended the terrain, Channing's leg ached in the spot where he hurt it while chasing Mayton.

"We'll call Harris and tell him the department needs to keep the protective detail on Pinkston. Mayton must have thought we would assume he's dead and let our guard down, at least until DNA tests show that he didn't die here tonight."

Channing did not speak. He did not like it when pieces were missing from a puzzle. In the brief time since Mayton was identified as the killer, they had learned his wife, Cindy, had died a horrible death as cancer ate away at her body. By the time she passed away, she was a faint echo of her former self, too weak to get out of bed, and bald from hopeless treatments. Channing wondered about Wayland's scalping. Was the removal of his hair meant to be symbolic of the effects of chemotherapy as opposed to a reference to Washington's Landing? Did it matter? And where the hell was Abdella killed? Wayland was killed in his home; Culligan was murdered in a parking garage; but nobody had uncovered the Abdella scene. Then a thought occurred to Channing.

"We need to head back downtown."

"To the station?" asked Lambert.

"No. We need to go to where it all started."

– – –

Cigarette smoke wafted from her mouth and flowed up his nostrils. Stifling a cough, Mayton did his best to ignore her. The newscast on the television above the bar was nearly inaudible, but the caption at the bottom of the screen held the most important piece of information.

Suspect in Killing of City Officials Believed Dead.

Another blast of smoke crossed his line of sight. If smoking in places like this had been banned, nobody in here seemed to care. There were a handful of people in the bar. He wished the woman beside him would gravitate toward one of them. He reached up and rubbed a hand over his newly shaven head and then adjusted the recently purchased eyeglasses that had useless lenses.

The haggard woman said, "Now, hockey—that's a real sport. Football is great, but it's gotten too soft."

Mayton took another sip of the drink sitting on the bar. He had come in here to simply watch the news and confirm his plan had succeeded, but from the bartender's tone, it became apparent that he was expected to order a drink. Not knowing if he could tolerate any other type of alcohol, he turned to the bartender and said, "Give me something with rum in it." Now, he was drinking a rum and Coke and becoming increasingly annoyed at the decrepit creature that had taken a seat next to him. From the minute he walked in, she had focused her attentions on him—occasionally touching his arm and licking her lips.

"It used to be a real game, back in the sixties and

seventies. You didn't hear the players whine about concussions and all that nonsense. You know what I mean?"

Mayton stared at the television and strained to hear the reporter's voice. From what he could tell, the terminally ill Danny Berres had done his job. Mayton had known that, compared to the physical suffering Berres was going through, the pain of knowing his elderly mother would go uncared for weighed heavily on him. With no other living relatives and his money all but gone, Berres was exhilarated when Mayton had reached in his coat and handed him a sizable check. It was enough money to ensure Berres' mother would be well cared for in the years to come.

Berres did not react particularly well when Mayton explained to him what would have to be done to earn the money. He told Berres an elaborate lie about how Treva Pinkston was using her position with City Planning to shut down any facilities that focused on helping those who are HIV-positive, including the New Heights Outreach Center. Mayton told him how Pinkston had garnered major support in the city government, and drastic action had to be taken. Mayton suggested the best way for Berres's life to mean something, was to martyr himself in a protest against the city. He was to approach Pinkston's house, wait for her security people to discover him, and then set himself ablaze. Mayton could only make out portions of the news broadcast, but it appeared Berres panicked and ran as far as his weakened condition would allow. However, in the end, he had done as instructed. From the caption on the screen, Berres had also failed to notice Mayton's wallet stuffed in a pocket of the gym bag that he thought also contained burglary tools. Berres never doubted Mayton's word that he would later send an anonymous email to all the major media outlets, explaining the noble reasons for Berres's actions and pleading for the community to take up his cause. Mayton felt no sympathy for the man. Berres had wanted to die and Mayton was happy to help speed up the process.

"Hey—are you listening to me?"

Without looking at her—he could not bear to look at this ragged, filthy person—he said, "I don't follow sports. I'm trying to listen to the TV."

The woman, who was no stranger to being ignored, took offense at what was obviously a brush off. She leaned in toward Mayton. The smell of stale Marlboros and beer intruded into his space. She gave him a nudge on the shoulder and said, "No sports, huh? What are you, some sort of fag?"

"Leave me alone."

Speaking to the bartender, who she seemed to know well, she said, "Hey, Walter! Are you turning this place into a bar for queers?"

Mayton stood to leave and placed cash on the bar.

The woman looked up at him and said, "Maybe you just need a real woman," while she simultaneously grabbed his crotch.

Before the woman could react, he grabbed a clump of her hair and slammed her head into the oak bar. He repeated the action four more times until the woman went limp and stopped screaming. The bartender reached under the bar, pulled out an aluminum baseball bat, and took a swing at the bald man, who was deceptively fast and strong. Mayton leaned back and watched the bat fly past his nose, and then lunged at his attacker. Grabbing the man's shirt with one hand and an abandoned beer bottle with the other, Mayton broke the bottle against the bar and then plunged it into the bartender's throat. The man's eyes registered shock as blood poured from his ruptured carotid artery. He dropped to the floor with a thud as Mayton turned toward the patrons seated at the tables in the middle of the room. Blood dripped from the broken glass in Mayton's hand. When nobody dared to approach him, Mayton dropped the bottle and walked out the exit. He had never felt so alive. He had never felt so powerful. He had never felt so…godlike.

— — —

The tapping on the glass caused Marvin McKeand to bolt upright in his chair at the reception desk. Standing on the other side of the glass doors, two individuals displayed badges. Using a plastic access card, the guard unlocked the lobby door for the detectives. Aside from the occasional security guard, the main offices for the city's Housing Authority, as well as all the other government offices located on Washington's Landing, were all but abandoned at this time of night.

The stocky African-American man in the signature gray Stillwell Security uniform said, "Is there a problem, officers? I don't think we had any alarms go off."

Channing replied, "No problems. We're sorry to bother you, but we were wondering if you always work at this building."

"Yes, sir. I've been on midnights here ever since I started with the company a few months ago."

"Have you noticed anything suspicious?"

McKeand stroked his chin and said, "Suspicious? No. This is a quiet gig. In fact, other than the townhome community, the island is pretty much deserted at night."

Lambert asked, "Have you noticed anyone unusual hanging around?" Pulling out a picture of Mayton, she said, "Maybe this guy?"

"Nope. Like I said, it's quiet here at night. And I read all the dayshift reports and nobody has reported anything."

Channing was feeling deflated, but kept grasping at straws. "Have any employees reported having any problems? Anyone been threatened or harassed?"

"Is this about Mr. Abdella?" asked McKeand. "He was such a nice man. Sometimes, he'd get here early, before my shift was over, and always stopped to chat it up. Nice man. Hard worker, too." McKeand smiled at a memory. "Sometimes the man would be preoccupied and pop in the side door at four or five on a Sunday morning, forgetting the alarm on that door was armed on the weekend. He'd call down and apologize over and over again."

Channing turned to Lambert and gave a silent indication that it was time to go. The detectives' hopes sank as they began to turn away.

McKeand was still reminiscing. He said, "I didn't get to see him last Sunday. I sure wish I had gotten a chance to talk to him one last time."

The detectives stopped in their tracks. Lambert asked the security guard to repeat what he had said.

"He set the alarm off last Sunday. But he didn't call down that day."

Channing thought back to the medical examiner's report on Abdella. It had placed the time of death to be early Sunday morning.

He asked, "How do you know it was him?"

The guard's voice became tentative. "Well, it was always him. And I went and checked the door and it wasn't damaged. Mr. Abdella had used his access card and let himself in."

Lambert asked, "And you didn't check to make sure it was him?"

"Well...no...I mean, it was always him on Sunday mornings. And he's the boss, so I didn't want to call up there and...I mean...it had to be him, right?"

"Do you have security cameras?"

"Sure," said McKeand. "But not on the side door."

Lambert fired off more questions at the man who was becoming distressed. "When the access cards are used, does it register in a computer? Can you tell whose card was used?"

McKeand shook his head. "Our system doesn't work that way. All the cards are basically the same. But only employees are allowed to have a card."

"What about former employees?" asked Lambert.

"Anyone who isn't going to work here anymore is supposed to turn their card in to their supervisor. It's a rule."

"And is that rule always followed?"

The guard shrugged. "I don't know. I guess it's up to the person's supervisor. Look, we have a lot of respons—"

Channing cut him off. "Is any part of this building not in use?"

"There are offices on every floor. It's a busy place during the day."

"Are there any large storage areas, or sections being renovated?"

"No. It's a new building, there's nothing to renovate. And the storage areas are really just closets."

"And the basement?" asked Channing, not sure if he wanted to hear the answer.

"I don't know about that. There's a basement, but nobody

goes down there. I guess I don't know what's down there."

Channing's stomach turned as he said, "Let's go take a look."

On the walk down the stairs, beads of sweat formed on Channing's forehead. When the three were nearly halfway down the staircase, he hesitated and reached for a railing. Visions of chains and blades filled his mind. His mouth ached for a drink and his legs begged him to retreat. Reminding himself that Mayton could be hiding out in the basement, he took a deep breath and drew his weapon with his uninjured arm. Lambert was already prepared for a confrontation, GLOCK in hand, and was keeping one eye on her partner.

The security guard reached the door and swiped an access card across a scanner. He pushed the door open. A portable light in the corner of the room was fading, but laid out a path to the center of the basement. McKeand doubled over and vomited the second his eyes reached the end of the trail and the smell forced him to spin away. In the middle of the room sat a chair surrounded by blood and human excrement. Channing and Lambert used their flashlights to sweep the room for targets, then announced to each other that the room was clear. Lambert told the security guard to go wait in the lobby and watched him give a quick nod and flee up the stairs. She turned to see Channing lean back against the wall next to the stairs. He covered his mouth with the sleeve of his bandaged arm to filter out the odors in the room.

She said, "Let's go up and call this in. It will take the forensic guys a while to sort this out, but this has to be where Abdella was killed."

Her partner squatted down and pressed his back to the concrete wall. The light from the stairwell above him cast his shadow through the room. "I wonder what Abdella was thinking," he said between breaths. "I wonder if he begged. He had to know it would be useless to bargain with a man who had lost his wife. I wonder if he prayed—if he thought God might forgive him for what he and the others had done."

"We should get out of here," said Lambert.

Channing did not seem to hear her. "I tried to kill myself the morning before we met."

Lambert froze, not knowing what to say.

"I put my gun to my head and pulled the trigger. It was a misfire. The gun or the bullet in the chamber failed. It had never malfunctioned before—never."

Lambert spoke softly and said, "I know it's a cliché, but things happen for a reason."

Channing was still not looking at her. He was staring at the empty, bloody chair where Abdella had been butchered. "A few months ago, I would have laughed at you. Or, more likely, told you to go screw yourself. But now…"

He repositioned himself and took a seat on the stairs. He held his pistol up so it was in Lambert's view.

"I sent my GLOCK and the ammo I had to the department's armorer to see if he could fix it. This…" He rotated the gun side to side. "…is a replacement. He left me a message earlier today. He said the gun and the ammo checked out fine. He fired through all the ammunition I gave him and never had a misfire."

"So, what do you think that means?" asked Lambert.

Channing reached back and violently holstered his weapon. "I think there really is a reason some things happen. I think events can consume us, but don't have to define us. I think I came out of that damned basement because my work in this world isn't complete. But you know what else? I think

Mayton is still in town and he's not running. No, he's not running and he's not hiding. He's lying in wait. He knows he's running out of time, but he knows we are, too. I don't completely understand the reason for me being alive, but if I had to take a guess, I'd say stopping Lester Mayton from hurting anyone else is as good a reason as any."

– – –

The squad room was buzzing with activity long before sunrise. Through the night, the forensics team had processed the scene at the Housing Authority building. Channing and Lambert walked into the flurry of activity, unsure of the reason for the excitement. The only radio traffic they heard on the drive back to the station related to a double-homicide at a bar on the South Side.

Sadly, a customer killing a bar patron and the bartender were hardly the cause for this much commotion these days. Exhausted and having planned only to file hastily written reports before heading to their respective homes, the detectives sought out their sergeant and found him in his office. Harris was barking orders into the phone and furiously writing notes on a legal pad. Hanging up the phone and standing, he kept scribbling and did not notice his visitors.

"Ken," Channing said. "What's happened?"

"The mayor's wife called. He went out for a jog this morning and didn't come back. His car was found at the park where he usually runs. A dog walker said they saw a man being shoved into a white van."

"Where was his protection detail?" asked Lambert.

A realization hit Channing and he slumped into a chair and proposed an answer to the question. "Because, the detail was dropped when Mayton's ID and weapons were found on the body outside the Pinkston residence."

"It wasn't dropped by us," said Harris angrily. "Mayor Wirrer insisted it wasn't necessary. He called the chief and put a halt to all protective details."

Lambert took the seat in the chair next to her partner and said, "Why the mayor? I thought this was about Washington's Landing."

"Son of a bitch!" Channing erupted and held his head in his hands. "I'm an idiot."

"What?" asked Lambert.

"Mayor Wirrer wasn't *Mayor* Wirrer back when the Washington's Landing project started."

"My God," said Harris, falling back into his own chair. "He was the head of City Planning."

STEP 12

Having had a spiritual awakening as a result of these steps, we tried to carry this message to addicts, and to practice these principles in all our affairs.

Six hours passed with no developments in the search for the city's highest elected official. The squad room had been turned into a command post for the largest search operation the area had ever seen. All attempts to shut out media coverage had failed and reporters flooded the streets around the station, all asking the same question: *Is Lester Mayton alive and has he abducted the mayor?* Adding to the confusion, witnesses from the South Side's double-homicide were telling detectives that the suspect in those killings had been intently watching news coverage of the attempted attack on the city's Planning Director. While the witnesses described a man with a clean-shaven head and glasses, when the sketch artist had finished her work, there were obvious similarities between the suspect and Lester Mayton. Fingerprints from the broken beer bottle left at the scene matched those found in Mayton's home, all but confirming he was the perpetrator.

Channing and Lambert had sought refuge from the squad room and set up shop in a conference room. Spread out on the table were stacks of reports, crime scene photos, statements from Mayton's friends and neighbors, and the killer's financial records. Teams of detectives had dissected the life of Lester Mayton in the hours after the SWAT team found his house was empty. Lambert was pouring over the piles of information at one end of the table, hoping to find some clue as to where the mayor's abductor would have taken him. At the other end of the table, Channing had his head buried in a laptop computer as he continued to sift through the hundreds of calls that had come into the department's tip line. Lambert glanced up and saw gut-wrenching distress in her partner's expression.

"You couldn't have known," she said in an even tone.

Channing moved a finger up to the monitor and kept scrolling through the logs. He should have seen this coming. Mayton never intended to get away with anything. He was just buying time. Now he either had killed or was preparing to kill the mayor and it was Channing's fault. *This can't be the reason I'm here,* he thought. *I can't still be alive just so I'll have to endure more punishment. If I can't make this right, how can I make anything right? I've known this man from the beginning. I've felt his pain. I have to end this. Nobody else. Me.*

Seeing her comment had not made a dent, Lambert frowned and returned to the interview notes in her hand. Another detective, a woman from Robbery, had interviewed some of Mayton's former coworkers. According to the notes, Mayton had few friends and no hobbies. Besides attending church and volunteering at an outreach center, he appeared to be a reclusive individual. Officers were already searching the outreach center and the church.

Without looking up, she said, "Do you want to go out there and see if the search parties found anything?"

When she did not get a response, she turned and discovered she was talking to empty space. While she was engrossed in the interview notes, he must have slipped out of the room. Remembering the agonizing look on his face, and fearing he may have sneaked out for a drink, she decided she would give him no more than ten minutes before tracking him down.

After enough time had passed, she walked into the squad room and searched for her partner. Having no luck, she pounded on the door of the men's room and then verified Channing was not in there. She made a circuitous trip through the hallways surrounding the squad room and became more concerned about the man who had discussed suicide less than twelve hours before. Lambert withdrew her cell phone and called Channing, only getting his voice mail.

She returned to the conference room, stopped to gather her thoughts, and then fixed her eyes on the laptop Channing had been using. No more than ten tip line entries appeared on the screen, and none of them had been investigated. She scrutinized them one at a time. The first four were obviously calls from conspiracy theorists. The fifth appeared to be from a psychic who stated the murderer was a Chinese man in a blue Volkswagen. The sixth entry made her pause and reread the words several times. She looked at the date and time of the entry. The call had been received early in the morning on the day Abdella's body came down the Duquesne Incline.

According to the call log, an anonymous caller stated he had received a call from a troubled soul and the caller feared something terrible was about to happen. The caller also stated, "The man is in pain and may be off the path. I fear he will make the city feel his loss. Please protect those in power." The caller refused to identify himself or the man to whom he was referring. Lambert's finger traced the row of the spreadsheet to the far right edge of the screen until she found what she was looking for. The department's caller-ID had captured the phone number.

Lambert, her pulse racing, pressed the keys on her cell phone.

"Hello," said a man's voice.

"This is Detective Lambert with the Pittsburgh Police."

"I'm sorry, but like I said before, I've already done all I can."

"Sir, please don't hang up," she said. "I think you may know the man who has killed all these people. We need your help."

"I've already explained my predicament. You know I'm in a tough situation here."

Predicament? Lambert adjusted the laptop's monitor and read the entry for the fourth time.

She said, "I don't understand. Whoever you spoke to on the tip line didn't explain any predicament."

"I didn't mention it on the tip line. I told the man who called a few minutes ago. What was his name? Channing."

Lambert felt blood rush through her body. She said, "Please forgive me, mister…"

The man hesitated to speak, but then said, "Ponstville. Matthew Ponstville."

"Please forgive me, Mr. Ponstville. Detective Channing is my partner, but I can't reach him right now. Can you please repeat to me what you told him?"

Another pause filled the air, and then the man answered, "I explained I can't give you the man's name, but I'm very concerned for him and for those he may still harm."

"Do you know the man's name?" the detective asked.

"Yes."

"But you won't give it to me."

"I'm not permitted."

Lambert felt anger begin to rise. "What does that mean, 'not permitted'?"

"As I explained to your partner, I'm a minister. In fact, some of your officers were here asking to search my church a few minutes ago. Of course, I let them.

Ponstville began coughing. To Lambert, he sounded elderly and frail. The coughing slowly subsided and he continued his story.

"The man called me early one morning and said he was on top of Mt. Washington. He said he had done things people would consider terrible. He asked if I thought God would understand what he was doing."

"And your duty to the church is keeping you from revealing his name to us."

"Yes."

"What else did you tell Detective Channing?"

"I told him that the man who called me was not a bad man. I said he had suffered a tremendous loss and how nearly the only thing that brought him pleasure in this life was gone."

"His wife."

Dead air filled the phone.

"You said *nearly* the only thing."

"Other than church and his volunteer work, he has few interests."

"Mr. Ponstville," said Lambert. "We know the man is Lester Mayton and we need to find him now. He's obviously not at the church and not at the outreach center. I can tell you want to help and I sympathize with your situation, but we think he has the mayor and is going to kill him."

"I'm sorry, dear. I don't know what else to tell you. I don't think I was much help to your partner either. I told him all I could about the man without breaking my vow of confidentiality. I'm ashamed to say I don't know that much about him. Like I told your partner, other than coming to church and helping the sick at some clinic, I don't know what he does in his spare time. He once mentioned he would occasionally dress up as a settler, or colonist, or something like that, but I'm not sure why. Your partner seemed interested in that for some reason."

By the time Ponstville realized the call had gone dead, Lambert was sprinting toward her car.

During the night, overcast skies and a northern wind had blown heavy snow down from the Great Lakes. Channing listened to the cool blanket of whiteness compress and creak under his feet. Beside his feet, a set of tire tracks were vanishing beneath new flakes. A chain that stretched across the entrance to the historical attraction had been broken, apparently pulled to its limits by the front of a car. Channing's eyes followed the tracks past the shattered chain. Overhead, a handmade wooden sign read, *Welcome to Historical Pioneer Village*. Below it, a smaller sign that swung from hooks read, *Winter Hours: 9:00 a.m.—4:00 p.m. / Saturday, Sunday, Monday, and Tuesday, and By Appt*. Channing decided to leave his car at the entrance and follow the tracks into the complex. It was Wednesday, but he was certain he had an appointment.

Located along the banks of the Ohio River, the village was nestled in an isolated area northwest of the city. Any concerns

Channing had about jurisdictional lines, swept away with the frigid winds. The detective drew his service weapon with his functional left hand, held it at his side, and took cautious steps into the late eighteenth century.

On his left, stood log structures and signs that advertised a courthouse, a rope maker's business, a general store, and a blacksmith shop. To his right, Channing observed stables and what looked like a saloon. In front of Channing, the tire marks continued with no indication the vehicle had stopped.

Another gust of wind intruded the replica town, and the coldness caused his gun hand to sting. Channing had not been completely honest with his partner. He could shoot left-handed, but not particularly well. Now with withdraw symptoms sending tremors down through his fingertips, he doubted he could hit anything at all. A deer sauntered across the road in front of him. Channing did not react and kept moving, occasionally swiveling his head from side to side. He forced his eyes up into the wind to look at the second story of a log house, but saw no movement in any windows. Pressing forward, the realization he was going to die in this place overcame him. Strangely, that knowledge consoled him. He felt no desire to escape his fate.

As he passed a building labeled as a gunsmith shop, Channing noticed footprints next to the tire tracks that continued through the town. Channing's eyes strained to make out the shapes on the ground as the skies darkened from dense clouds. To the detective, it appeared that the driver had stopped the car and walked to and from the shop before continuing his journey in the vehicle. Channing approached the door of the shop and took notice of the splintered lock.

Without bothering to raise his weapon, Channing nudged

the door open with his foot. A low-pitched squeak came from the hinges and the door reluctantly swung open. Stepping in, he allowed time for his eyes to adjust to the blackness as floorboards ached underneath his weight. The shop was small and simple. A counter stood on one side of the room while crates and barrels filled the other. Channing followed traces of moisture from footsteps left not long before. The trail ended in a corner of the room. The detective knelt down and could make out a faint circle outline in the dust on the floor; a barrel had been recently removed and loaded into the vehicle.

Channing stood and walked back to the damaged door. *This wasn't part of the plan, was it, Mayton? This was a last minute decision. You're improvising. You've gone off script. Like killing those people in the bar—you've come unglued and now you're making it up as you go along.* He returned to the road and picked up his pace as the tire tracks became indistinguishable from the surrounding landscape.

The road—at least Channing assumed it was still a road— led him into a remote, wooded tract of land west of village. He could no longer follow the tracks, so he looked for the areas where a car might be able to squeeze between trees. The wind picked up. Clumps of snow fell from the canopy of branches overhead and pockmarked the peaceful terrain. Channing arrived at a small clearing and halted. On three different sides were gaps large enough to allow a vehicle to pass.

No, he thought as he closed his eyes. *This can't be how this ends. In the past few months, I've failed everyone around me: God, Mary, Alex…myself. My life is not without value and neither will be my death. I have to balance the scales and make things right.*

Channing opened his eyes and watched plump flakes drift

downward, contrasting with the stillness of the scene. More than a minute passed before he thought he heard something. He heard it again. The insulation of the snow and the occasional wind gust made it difficult to determine a direction. Then, he heard it again. It sounded like a cry of pain. It was a sound Channing knew all too well. The sound reached him twice more before he decided on the path to his right. Moving as swiftly as the ground allowed, he ran until he spotted a diminutive building at the edge of a clearing. Channing assumed the building was some sort of maintenance building or groundskeeper's office. The village would hardly want a modern day groundskeeper walking among volunteers dressed in 1790s attire. Channing realized the village would have little use for a groundskeeper during the winter. The structure could make for a nice little hideout for someone trying to stay out of sight.

The window facing Channing was vacant. No smoke rose from the stovepipe chimney. Beside it sat a white van with a license plate number Channing had memorized not long after he first heard the name of Lester Mayton. Channing surveyed his surroundings, making sure he was not walking into a trap. His eyes spotted a squirrel scavenging for acorns. He watched as the creature found its treasure and scampered behind a corner of the building. Raising his eyes from where the contented squirrel had vanished, he looked back to the window. Two eyes blazed back at him. Without presenting the slightest hint of alarm, Lester Mayton's face gradually receded into the blackness.

The window remained empty as Channing walked to the door. By the time he reached the door, the tremors had left his hands. For the first time in a long time, a sense of clarity washed over him and he felt the air filling his lungs. A blizzard of good memories passed through his mind. He saw childhood friends, birthday parties, college cram sessions, Mary laughing, weddings, a badge pinned on his chest—

It's been more good than bad. Let it all define my life. All of it.

The rickety doorknob wobbled as it turned. He pushed the door open and took a step into the building's lone room. The small amount of daylight that managed to come through the window and open doorway did little to brighten the room. The only internal source of light came from the other side of the room where Mayton held a flickering candle in one hand. Mayton's other hand held a knife to the throat of a battered and bloody Mayor Marc Wirrer, seated and tied to a chair. The mayor was barely conscious, but alive.

"I'd hoped I would have more time," said Mayton.

Keeping the gun at his side, Channing took another half step into the room and felt snow shift around his feet. He saw that Mayton's eyes were sunken and his complexion pale. His shaven head and chiseled white face gave him a demonic quality. Whoever he was before, that man was dead.

"I had big plans for Mr. Wirrer. I was going to finish him off here and then take him to my boat, which is tied off near Washington's Landing. Since the river hasn't quite frozen over yet, I was going to anchor it off shore where his bloody corpse and I would stare at than infernal place until the crowds came. Then, it would all be over. I would have completed my mission and could peacefully slip overboard and let the river's icy waters take me to my sweet Cindy."

Mayton pulled the knife hard against Wirrer's throat, forcing the man's chin to move toward the ceiling. The mayor made a sound that was something between a grunt and a whine. "But I guess none of that is going to happen now, is it?" Mayton concluded.

"No, I guess not," said Channing, knowing that if Mayton's original plan did not include an escape strategy then he certainly did not have one now.

"You know, I saw you at the Incline," said Mayton. "I recognized you from the news reports after you got tortured and your partner was killed. I remember how the mayor and all those bastards threw your name around and lauded you as a hero, but I don't ever remember you giving an interview. Did you ever give interviews?"

"No."

"Why not?"

Channing did not answer. He shifted his weight and felt the snow again. Then, he finally noticed the smell of the room. It was a smell vaguely familiar to him. He looked down at his feet and realized the floor was not covered with snow.

"I didn't want to talk about it," Channing answered. "My partner was also my best friend. When you lost your wife, did you feel like talking about it?"

Channing shifted his eyes around the room and found the item he expected to see. Against a wall, next to a painting Channing vaguely recognized, was an open wooden barrel. Channing understood now. Every single inch of the floor was covered in gunpowder.

Seeing the detective had put it all together, Mayton said, "Please excuse the mess. When you chased me into that warehouse the other day, it made me realize I needed to take more precautions. For instance, if someone managed to find me out here, I could still make sure our friend the mayor didn't survive. I've covered the place with gunpowder and that barrel over there is still half full. Obviously, if I drop this candle, this all ends pretty quickly."

Answering Channing's previous question, Mayton said,

"As for me *losing* my wife. I didn't *lose* her. They took her!" Mayton pulled the knife harder, causing the mayor to scream. The candle in his other hand wobbled ominously. A slight breeze came through the open door behind Channing, causing the yellow flame to fight against the rush of air.

"Those men had to be punished. You know that in your heart," continued Mayton.

"Andy Lach didn't deserve to die," said Channing. "And what about those two people you killed at the bar. I heard you crushed the woman's skull."

Mayton grew solemn at the mention of those deaths. Channing saw the slight change in expression and decided to press the issue.

"And how about whoever that poor bastard was that you convinced to set himself on fire?"

Channing's mistake became evident as Mayton's voice boomed through the small room. "He deserved what he got! All of those heathens at the center will burn eventually! And this devil has already admitted to me about how he worked with Culligan, Abdella, and Wayland to cover up my wife's murder. So, now I'm going to send him straight to Hell with the rest of them."

Channing tried to change tactics. "Killing the mayor won't bring your wife back. Let him go and I'll stay here with you. Before long, the news crews will be rolling in and you can tell the world what he did. You can tell the world what all of them did."

Mayton looked at Channing with a mixture of fury and amazement and yelled, "Do you think I give a damn what the world thinks right now? The message may not be understood for a while. For the time being, this is about debt collection and settling accounts. This is about equaling things out. This is about balancing the scales and making things right. You have no idea what it feels like to know you failed someone and you can never make things up to her! You have no idea what loss is!"

Channing stood in disbelief as Mayton sprayed words that seemed all too familiar to him. Mayton felt something change in the room and watched his adversary with curiosity and wariness.

With a deep sense of resignation, Channing looked into Mayton's eyes and said, "There's nothing I can do to convince you to let him go, is there?"

Without a word, Mayton drew the knife across Wirrer's throat. Blood poured from the fatal wound. The detective raised his gun, but did not fire. A bullet would not solve anything. Channing and Mayton locked eyes as the mayor ineffectually gasped for air. In less than a minute, he was gone.

Mayton was the first to speak. "It's over. You should go now. Don't worry; I won't be leaving this building."

Channing was devastated and speechless. He did not know what outcome he had expected, but this was not it. He had failed—again. He let someone die—again. The man standing in front of him was responsible for eight deaths and he was simply going to…what? Blow himself up and leave nothing behind but pain and suffering. He would get to leave this world while others had to struggle every day to pick up the pieces of shattered lives.

"We're both leaving," said Channing.

Mayton glanced at the art print leaning on the wall. "I thought I might have killed you in that warehouse. And honestly, I didn't care. But when I saw you standing outside just now, I was actually glad you were still alive. Regardless of what master you serve, you know what pain is, don't you? Who better to tell the story?"

"We're both leaving," repeated Channing, his weapon pointed at the chest of his adversary. "One way or another."

"You don't fear death, Detective?"

"No."

"I don't either. It always seemed silly to fear the unknown."

"I agree," said Channing flatly.

Mayton unintentionally lowered the candle as he said, "What do you fear?"

Channing thoughts took him back to the moment he tasted the barrel of his own gun. The hard click of the of the trigger pull still echoed in his ears. He thought of his unquenchable thirst to forget everything. To erase everything.

"I feared life," said Channing.

"But no longer?"

"It seems silly to fear the unknown."

"I agree," said Mayton, a slight grin crossing his lips.

"If you drop that candle, you will have even more blood on your hands."

Mayton nodded. His face was ghostly and peaceful. "That's my cross to bear. You have five seconds."

In a resolute tone, Channing said, "You don't get a free pass. I'm taking you out of here."

Channing, silhouetted by the open door, stepped forward quickly. Without hesitation, Mayton raised the knife. From behind Channing, a shot rang out and struck the murderer in the chest. Channing watched the burning candle drop in slow motion. A carpet of flame consumed the room and raced toward the barrel of gunpowder. Channing whipped his head around to the door. Lambert was standing in a perfect firing stance, her GLOCK still smoking in the cold air. She saw a killer threaten her partner with a knife and fired center-mass. There was no way for her to know she was lighting the fuse of a bomb.

In three powerful strides, Channing threw himself into Lambert's chest, knocking the wide-eyed woman back into the snow. Simultaneously, a scream of pain erupted from inside the shed. Before Lambert could process what was happening, Channing draped the entirety of his beaten, scarred body over her and somehow pressed her further into the frigid earth. To her, the blast that followed felt like a sledgehammer to the heart.

EPILOGUE

Tina Lambert liked coming out here. There was something very tranquil about the rural countryside of western Pennsylvania. She had never imagined Channing would choose to end up in this place. A hawk was enjoying the warm spring day and soared above her as she walked down the gravel path. Flowers lined both sides of a walkway that was not accustomed to seeing many visitors. Something about this place made her listen to the buzzing of the insects and the singing of the birds. Somehow, her visits here helped her put things in perspective.

As she neared the end of the path, an inharmonious hammering followed by a jagged-sounding curse disrupted her meditative state. She smiled widely and headed toward the source of the noise.

The door to the detached garage was open. She stood and surveyed the disaster zone spread out in this makeshift workshop. Channing—a hammer in one hand and a swollen thumb on the other—was muttering a string of curses and stomping a foot. His silent visitor covered her mouth and stifled a laugh.

Without turning, Channing said, "Well, are you going come in and visit, or just stand there and make fun of me?"

"Can't I do both?" she asked, noticing the burn marks and scars from the blast were still visible on the back of his neck.

Channing put the offending tool on top of some slats of wood, walked over, and hugged his former partner.

"You don't come out here nearly enough," said Channing.

"So, you miss me?"

Channing fixed a fake scowl on his face. "Not at all. But Mary says I need to have more friends and you are one of the few people who can put up with me."

"And she made you set up shop out here, away from the house. She's a smart woman," said Lambert, knowing the real reason he had his workshop in the garage was because the only other option was the house's basement.

Channing rolled his eyes and shrugged in exaggerated exasperation. "Most of them are." His eyes dropped to the thick binder she held in her right hand. In a playfully scolding tone, he said, "Ah, Tina, I told you I'm not interested."

"I know, I know. But I thought maybe you'd take a look at the case file and let me know if you have any general observations."

"Uh-huh," he responded, not believing the new sergeant of the Homicide Squad for a second.

It had been nearly a year since the Mayton case was officially closed. The blast that ended the life of Lester Mayton left Channing with second-degree burns and multiple shrapnel injuries. Lambert emerged from the wreckage with only minor cuts and bruises. The bomb squad and forensics experts determined that both of the detectives would have died were they standing at the time of the blast.

For Channing, the most disturbing part of the aftermath may have been waking up in the hospital to Backhoe's ugly face hovering over him and yelling, "Dude! You have to stop doing this! I hate coming to hospitals!" After a couple of days, Channing was sent home, having received an assortment of stitches and finally getting a cast on his broken right wrist. Lambert drove him home and relentlessly harassed him to call his wife. That evening he picked up the phone and dialed. He heard three rings—just three. Then, two words changed everything. "Hello, Jackson."

Lambert followed Channing as he returned to his workbench and lined up a piece of wood next to a circular saw. "Like you said, you don't have many friends. Maybe you can help us out on a cold case and it will keep you busy."

"I didn't say that. Mary is the one who said that. But I have plenty of friends."

"Name five," Lambert dared.

Channing acted like he was focusing on the project in front of him and said, "Well...there's you. There's Backhoe..." Channing scratched his head. "And Jack."

Lambert took a step closer.

In a worrisome tone, she said, "Jack? You don't...not..."

It took Channing a second to understand her concern. He laughed loudly. "He's our cat! Mary got us a cat. And no, his last name isn't Daniels."

Lambert sighed and grinned at her mistake.

"So, see. I've got plenty of friends," said Channing.

Her tone was sincere now. "How are you doing...really?"

Channing faced her and said, "I'm doing very well. I'm not drinking. I'm going to AA. I'm running three times a week. Mary has been great." He pointed to the partially completed carpentry project next to his feet. "And obviously we are moving forward."

Lambert lifted the binder and said, "I would understand you leaving and taking disability if you just had enough of the job. But you left because you blame yourself for Wirrer's death. Wirrer was dead the minute he crossed Mayton. You know that, right?"

Channing did not answer.

"You can't save everybody," she said.

"I didn't save anybody," said Channing.

"You saved me," she said while putting a hand on his shoulder. "And in doing so, you saved yourself. You count, too. If that's not enough, since you left the department, I've put several more murderers away. Many were sociopaths who would have killed again and again. It's a chain reaction, Jackson. Things happen for a reason."

He knew she was right, but part of him could not—or would not—accept everything she was saying. How was it that an ounce of bad always seemed to outweigh a ton of good? And now, she was here with a cold case she supposedly needed help in solving. It was a thinly veiled attempt to keep him busy and to give him some other avenue for redemption. All the same, he appreciated her efforts.

"Do you want to stay for dinner? I'll throw some steaks on the grill," said Channing.

"I'll have to take a rain check. I have to get back to the city," she replied while standing on her toes and giving him a friendly kiss on the cheek. "I'll call you next week and we can set something up. Tell Mary that I said hello, and take care of yourself."

Channing heard the sound of her footsteps soften as she walked down the path to the front of the house that he and Mary purchased a few months earlier. Mary thought a change of scenery would be good for both of them, and she had not been wrong. It was serene out here. He inhaled deeply and his eyes took in his surroundings. It was a beautiful afternoon and he was standing in his own workshop, surrounded by things that would let him create something. Jack walked in and jumped onto a sun-filled window ledge. He licked a paw, then stretched himself out for a nap. Everything Channing needed was laid out in front of him: a circular saw, a hammer, wood glue, a... binder. Channing's shoulders slumped. *I really wish I could hate her,* he thought, knowing it was a lie.

He grabbed the binder and looked at it. Paper tabs marking various pages protruded from the side and he read the tiny letters printed on the top tab. It read, *Person of Interest: Keller, Cyprus.* The name sounded somehow familiar and he started to open the binder, but stopped himself and tossed it aside. Jack's head shot up at the disturbance. "We'll see. We'll see," Channing said to his feline friend.

He took hold of the round piece of unfinished wood in front of him and lined it up parallel with the edge of the table. He wanted to get this finished before he even thought about diving into anything else. Channing knew that for all his talents, he was a terrible carpenter. He had been at this for a month and it would be weeks before he finished. It did not matter. He had seven more months until the baby was due. He could take his time building the crib. Looking around at the misshapen and mangled scraps of wood all around him, he thought about what Lambert had said about the chain reaction of good deeds. Perhaps he did help some people. Perhaps he still could. He thought about the cuts on his body and the surgeries that repaired them. *Some cuts kill and others heal,* he thought. Channing carefully stretched a tape measure along the piece of wood before him. *Whatever happens,* he thought, *I'm getting this one right.* He measured once. He measured twice.

###

ACKNOWLEDGMENTS

I am in debt to many people who have had a hand in getting *Measure Twice* from the manuscript stage through the publication process. Although it would be impossible to list the names of all of those who have been involved, I do want to recognize a few individuals who helped keep me on track.

As always, my wife Kasia has been incredibly patient and supportive. She is always there for me and is my partner in all things. Les Denton and Deborah Riley-Magnus with Assent Publishing and their imprint Bad Day Books were wonderful to work with and provided a great deal of support. Their patience and insight are greatly appreciated. I would also like to thank Dr. Gretchen Hartz who assisted me by answering my never-ending stream of medical questions regarding alcoholism and addiction. I would also like to thank Jeff Hartz for his continued assistance with maintaining my website and enduring my constant requests for changes and updates.

Additionally, I thank the incredibly supportive people in

the Pittsburgh area. Over the years, I have approached many individuals with countless research questions and I cannot recall ever being turned away. I should point out that in *Measure Twice* I make mention of a particular historical location on the outskirts of Pittsburgh. While the site in the book is fictitious, it is inspired by an actual historical attraction in the same area. In the book, I portrayed the location in a certain manner for purposes of the story, not due to any errors in research.

Finally, while *Measure Twice* is a thriller, it is ultimately a story about the struggle within and the search for redemption. I thank all of the heroes—many in my hometown of Huntington, West Virginia—who have battled and conquered their own demons and addictions. Their stories are more complex than could ever be represented in a simple novel. I apologize for not being able to pay tribute to those who have fought the good fight in a more meaningful way.

ABOUT THE AUTHOR

J.J. Hensley is a former police officer and Special Agent with the U.S. Secret Service who has drawn upon his experiences in law enforcement to write stories full of suspense and insight. Hensley graduated from Penn State University with a B.S. in Administration of Justice and has a M.S. degree in Criminal Justice Administration from Columbia Southern University. The author is currently a training supervisor with the U.S. Office of Personnel Management and lives with his beautiful wife, daughter, and two dogs near Pittsburgh, Pennsylvania.

Mr. Hensley's novel RESOLVE was named one of the BEST BOOKS OF 2013 by Suspense Magazine and was named a finalist for Best First Novel by the International Thriller Writers organization.

He is a member of the International Thriller Writers and Sisters in Crime.

Please visit J.J. Hensley online

https://hensleybooks.wordpress.com
www.hensley-books.com
www.facebook.com/hensleybooks
Twitter: @JJHensleyauthor
www.goodreads.com/jjhensley
amazon.com/author/hensleybooks

CPSIA information can be obtained at www.ICGtesting.com
Printed in the USA
BVOW05s1348120715

408375BV00010B/87/P